HIS BEST FRIEND'S WIDOW

HANNAH JO ABBOTT

To my readers,
who encourage me to keep writing and sharing the stories God
has laid on my heart.

H ailey Peterson hated being alone. She was afraid of the dark as a child and refused to sleep in her bed by herself. When she was older, she attached herself to friends, never wanting to go anywhere without someone.

These days it was hard to say she was alone in a house where three kids were running wild. That didn't mean she didn't feel lonely.

Hailey put one hand to her forehead as she used the other one to stir the taco meat on the stove. She used to say she could eat tacos every day. Tonight she wished for anything else, but tacos was one of the few meals she could guarantee her kids would eat without complaining, and tonight that was the only thing she could muster.

"Charlotte," Hailey called out to her oldest daughter. "Will you please set the table? Dinner will be ready in five minutes."

"Yes, ma'am," ten-year-old Charlotte responded as she

walked to the kitchen. Hailey didn't know what she would do without her.

Hailey tucked her shoulder-length brown hair behind one ear as she bit her lip. If Kyle were here, he could reach the bag of tortilla chips on the top shelf of the pantry. But with her short stature, Hailey needed a stool to climb up and reach. Once she retrieved them, she dragged herself to the refrigerator and pulled out a bag of shredded cheese, and containers of sour cream and salsa. Gone were the days of spending an hour in the kitchen, enjoying crafting a special meal for her family. It was all she could do to get a meal on the table and resist going through a drive-through on her way home from work.

Hailey brushed her hands down the front of her black dress pants, second-hand from her younger sister who gave her a box full of clothes when Hailey took a job. "Ellie and Carter, go wash your hands and come to the table." The two younger kids were playing a rowdy game in the living room and didn't even hear her. "Ellie," Hailey repeated to her eight-year-old daughter, "Go now." She paused and waited for her to respond. "Carter," Hailey raised her voice at the six-year-old who was now climbing over the back of the couch. "Get down from there. You know you're not supposed to do that." Hailey blew out a big breath. Her husband was the one who had let him play rough, even at a young age. After two girls, Hailey had wanted to let him have his buddy to wrestle with.

Now it was all just a big reminder that he wasn't here.

"Come on, guys," she tried to keep the frustration out of her voice, but it was a challenge. All she wanted was to collapse in bed and watch a movie, or maybe take a hot bubble bath with the lights down low. These days that was a pipe dream. By the time she got everyone fed, it would be baths, homework, and dishes. And once they were in bed, there would be laundry and making lunches for the next day. She'd heard the expression burning the candle at both ends, but she was pretty sure she was also melting in the middle.

"Mommy," Carter came up beside her and spoke in the sweet little voice that meant he was about to ask for something.

"Yes, buddy?"

"Can we have ice cream after dinner?" He smiled that million-dollar smile, and his eyes twinkled.

Hailey's heart twisted in a mixture of joy and sadness, seeing him look so much like his dad. "I don't think so. It's a school night, and we don't need that much sugar right before bed."

"So tomorrow?" Carter asked with a grin.

Hailey ruffled his hair. "Tomorrow is Friday, so maybe."

"Yes!" Carter jumped with a fist pumping in the air.

"Right now, go wash up for dinner."

"Yes, ma'am," Carter said, scampering off.

Hailey attempted a smile, but even her cheek muscles were too tired.

"Mom," Charlotte asked from the table where she was setting out plates and silverware. "Can I spend the night at Grandma's this weekend?"

Hailey tried to keep her face even and held in a sigh. "I'm not sure. I don't know if they have plans."

"Can I call and ask?" Charlotte asked, her voice full of excitement.

Hailey bit her lip. Charlotte didn't have to say it, but she knew it would be more fun at her grandparents' house. Weekends with Hailey were about catching up on everything they were behind on. Which was actually everything. There would be errands and extra cleaning and grocery shopping and laundry. What kid would want to hang around for that? "Not tonight," she answered Charlotte. "We'll talk about it tomorrow."

Charlotte rolled her eyes and dropped her shoulders. She probably guessed that Hailey meant no. She wanted to be able to let them go and have fun, but she would worry over them every second they were gone.

That seemed to be all she did these days. Worry about work, about money, about the kids' school, about feeding them enough vegetables. Worry that there wasn't enough of her to go around.

"Mama," Ellie came walking into the kitchen holding her hands high in the air. "Look, nice and clean." She beamed as she smiled at her mom. Unlike Carter, Ellie was like looking in a mirror. As the middle child, Ellie was the one always looking for approval, and Hailey hoped and prayed every day she would know she was enough.

"Great job, Ellie girl." Hailey turned and reached for the condiments. "Will you take these to the table? I'll bring the meat, and we can fix our tacos over there."

"Can I eat mine on chips?" Ellie asked.

"Yes, you can. Come on now, scoot."

Hailey forced a smile as her little family gathered

around the table. She bowed her head as the kids closed their eyes, and she thanked God for their food. She didn't say what she wanted to, though. That she was thankful that they all made it home safely to eat dinner together.

And that she would never get over that her husband hadn't done the same.

~

LANDON RICHARDS WAS MADE FOR THIS. HE TAPPED HIS fingers on the boardroom table during the meeting that was lasting way beyond five o'clock. He didn't care. This was an exciting project, and he was thrilled to be part of it. If he played his cards right, this could be the one that got him the promotion he'd been working toward for two years.

"Richards, you have the projections on the marketing budget?"

"Right here," Landon said, reaching into the manila file folder his assistant had put the printouts in. He could feel the approval emanating from his boss from across the table. Yes, he was doing everything right. He cleared his throat and began explaining the numbers on the spreadsheet that he passed around the table. "I think the clients will be very pleased with what we've done. I've already spoken to Mr. Jenkins, and he has other projects for us when we finish this one." Landon ran his hand over his neatly trimmed beard. It reminded him that he needed a haircut this weekend. His dark brown hair was creeping over his ears.

"Good work, Richards," his boss said.

Landon sat back in his seat and crossed his arms over his chest. It was good work, and he had worked hard for it. Benton Marketing Solutions Firm was the only place Landon had worked. When he graduated from college, he thought he might be like other guys he had grown up with who stayed in their home town and worked a regular nine-to-five. But he wanted more. Sure, he still lived in Twin Creeks, but it was only a forty-five minute drive to town. Scoring a job at a large company had always been the goal, and now he was set to decide his own path if things kept going well. Moving from a junior marketing assistant up to an assistant account manager had kept him busy, but he wasn't afraid to give even more time to move up in management. The firm had offices all over the country, and he loved the idea of traveling and living in different cities and always having a new adventure around the next corner.

When they finally wrapped up the meeting, Landon glanced at his watch. Eight-thirty. That was practically an early night. They had brought in takeout for the meeting, so now he could make it home and watch the basketball game he had set to record.

On the drive home, he watched as the big city buildings turned to more open land and then to the familiar main street lights in his small town. As much as he loved a new adventure, it would be hard to leave the only town he'd ever lived in, besides his four years of college in Nashville. There was something comforting about waving at people he knew as he drove through the main part of town. There was the local gossip mill too. He was pretty sure the older ladies were looking to set him up with a wife and convince him to settle down here.

That wasn't part of the plan.

Sure, Landon liked kids, and he was happy for his friends who had met their soulmate and were living their own happily ever afters.

But his ever after was his career.

As he drove past the neighborhood just before his, a memory stung his conscience like a mosquito bite in the middle of July.

Kyle's neighborhood.

How many times had he driven this road and turned down the street to his best friend's house? If he were still here, Landon might be turning there now, late as usual, to watch the basketball game together.

But he wasn't here. He never would be.

Just like so many times before tonight, he wondered how Hailey and the kids were doing. What if he pulled down the road and knocked on the door to check on them?

Landon grimaced. Hailey would probably shut the door in his face. No, maybe not. She didn't know that Landon was supposed to check in on them. He had made a promise to Kyle. But he'd done a terrible job at following through on that.

He remembered Hailey's face at the funeral. At the time, he had been too consumed with his own grief to say anything comforting, but the look on her face from that day was etched in his memory. He had told her he would be there if she needed anything. And then he went back to his own life.

Wouldn't it be awkward for him to call her now? It had been too long to jump back in. They had all been friends at one time, but what if he was just a reminder of Kyle that she didn't want?

No, tonight wasn't the time. Maybe he could send her a card. Did people still do that? Surely she could use some help. Maybe a gift card for a restaurant, so she could take the kids to dinner.

That was a good idea. He could ask his assistant to do that tomorrow.

Tonight, he would just get home. It was late anyway, for most everyone else. He would try to reach out tomorrow.

Then he could be one day further from losing his best friend, and the one happy family he had known.

2

Hailey ran through the doctor's office parking lot, stopping quickly to look both ways. She clutched each of the girls' hands in hers. "Come on, sweeties, we have to move quickly."

"Mama," Ellie said around a cough, "my ear hurts."

"I know, baby. I'm going to get you some medicine because the doctor said it's infected. I'm so sorry it hurts."

She had panicked when both girls woke up with fevers and coughs and called the doctor's office as soon as it was open. The earliest appointment available was at two o'clock in the afternoon, so they had suffered through the day. It meant Hailey had to miss work too. She cringed at the thought. How many days could she miss before they fired her? She tried her best to be a good employee, but what was she supposed to do when her kids were sick?

In the car, she made sure both girls were buckled before she pulled out of the parking lot and headed to the interstate. She hated that the doctor's office was on the other side of town from the kids' school, but they had been at the practice since they were babies, and she couldn't bear to change it.

Twenty minutes later, she slammed her fist against the steering wheel. "Why aren't we moving?" she said through gritted teeth. "We're going to be so late." She glanced at the clock and knew Carter would be waiting for them outside the school. At this rate, he would be the last kid there, and they might take him back into the office.

She couldn't let that happen.

Only once had she been late to pick him up. Right after they lost Kyle and she started her job, she misjudged the time to get to the school and they took him to the office. By the time she arrived, Carter was sobbing, worried something bad had happened to her too.

Reaching for her purse, she grabbed her phone and tried to think of who to call. Her parents were out of town. Maybe her sister could help. She pushed the button and listened to it ring over and over before she finally answered.

"Hey," Claire said, her voice sounding hoarse.

"Are you okay?" Hailey asked.

"Yeah, I mean, no, not really. I think I have the flu. I've been in bed all day."

"Oh no, I'm so sorry. I just took the girls to the doctor with coughs and fevers, but they're negative for the flu. I'll let you go."

"Did you need something?" Claire asked.

"Well, yes, I'm late to get Carter, and I'm stuck in traffic. But it's okay. Get some rest."

"I'm sorry."

Hailey barely heard her sister's words as she hung up

the phone. Who else could she call? If Kyle was here, she would have asked him to plan to pick Carter up before she even went to the doctor's appointment. She knew she wouldn't make it in time. But that didn't change the fact that there was no one to help today.

Kyle. Why can't you be here? You would probably be working from home today. It was Friday, and every other Friday the company let them work from home.

Working from home? Wouldn't Landon be working from home today? His house was five minutes from the elementary school.

No, she couldn't call him. She hadn't spoken to him in months, no more than a greeting as they passed each other at church. What would he think if she called him and asked for an emergency favor?

Hailey bit her lip as she looked at the clock again. Still, she was out of options, and she couldn't stand the thought of Carter standing on the sidewalk alone wondering where she was. She sighed and pressed the button on her phone to find his number.

After two rings, he answered. "This is Landon." His voice sounded professional and exactly like Kyle sounded when he was in full-on work mode. Maybe she shouldn't disturb him after all. Her voice seemed to catch in her throat. "Hello?" Landon asked.

"Hey, Landon, it's Hailey."

"Hey, what's up?" His tone changed to a more casual sound, and she realized he must not have her number in his phone. Why would he? He had been Kyle's friend, not hers.

"Are you at home? Or close to town, I mean?"

"Yep, I'm working at home today. Is everything okay?"

"Yes, sort of. I mean we're fine, but I'm late to pick up Carter from school because I had to take the girls to the doctor, and we're stuck in traffic on the interstate."

"Oh, gotcha." He cleared his throat. "Need me to go pick him up? Can I do that? Do I have to be on a list or something?"

"You're on the emergency list." She almost hated to admit it since he wasn't as close as they used to be. But last year when she needed to put another person down on the list, he was the person who came to mind.

"Oh, cool. Okay. No problem. I can leave now and be there in a few minutes. I'll just take him to your house and wait until you get there."

"Thanks, Landon. Oh, how will you get in the house?"

She could hear the smile in his voice. "I still have a key from that time y'all went out of town and asked me to feed the cat."

"Oh, right. Perfect. Sure, then, I'll just see you at the house as soon as I can."

"Later," Landon said before hanging up.

Hailey didn't know whether to breathe a sigh of relief or break down and cry. It was nice of Landon to jump to her aid, but she desperately wished she didn't need to ask.

"Who was that, Mommy?" Ellie asked.

"That was Mr. Landon."

"Mr. Landon?" Ellie scrunched her nose like she didn't know who that was.

Hailey sighed remembering that Landon never let them call him Mister. He said it made him feel old. Hailey had argued, but in the end, she'd lost that battle. "Landon," she repeated.

"You know," Charlotte said, "Daddy's friend, Landon."

"Oh," Ellie said, understanding dawning on her. "That Landon."

"We're running late, so Landon is going to pick up Carter at school and bring him home."

"Yay!" Ellie said. "Will we get to play?"

"Yeah, will we? Landon is funny," Charlotte said.

Hailey cracked a smile remembering his antics with the kids. Landon was funny and playful with the kids. "I don't know," she answered the girls. "Mr. Landon is very busy and has a lot of work to do. I don't know if he can stay very long."

That had to be true, didn't it? Landon must have stayed busy with work to stay away from them. He had told her to call if she needed anything, and today she had done that. But he had his own life. Sure, they had spent time with him before, but that was before they lost Kyle. She couldn't expect him to stay close with them when his best friend was gone.

No, she would thank him for his help today, and then she would try to plan better next time, so she didn't need to ask for help.

This was her life, and she had to figure out how to handle it on her own.

Since on her own was how it was going to be for the rest of her life.

3

L andon pulled into the driveway blasting country music through the speakers with the windows down.

Carter laughed as the wind blew through his hair, and he sang along to the music.

Landon glanced over his shoulder at the boy in time to see Hailey pull in behind him and park. Just in the nick of time. If she had beat them there, he was sure she would be worried sick, and he might be in trouble.

He stepped out of the car and waved. "Hey," he called out before reaching back into the car. "Took a little longer to get here because I stopped and picked up pizza." He held up the boxes as if they were a trophy.

"Oh," Hailey blinked rapidly. "Well, um, thanks. You didn't have to do that."

Landon shrugged as he opened the car door for Carter to climb out. "It was no big deal. I thought it might help out."

A look flashed across her face that he didn't quite

understand. Was it relief? Or fear? It was gone before he could decide, but he saw her touch her eyes quickly as if wiping away a tear.

"Thanks, Landon," she said. "That's a big help."

He breathed his own sigh of relief and moved toward the front door. He carried the pizza inside and set it on the table. Glancing around the room, the awkwardness hit him full swing. It had been a long time since he was in this house. He came over once after the funeral to drop off something. He couldn't remember what it was now. Something that he had borrowed from Kyle and felt like he should still return it. Now that seemed silly. Kyle didn't need it. Maybe Landon just needed it out of his house.

He cleared his throat as he noticed the pile of laundry on the couch, and the toys that littered the floor. All signs that a busy family lived here. He turned to face Hailey. "Are the girls sick?" He rubbed his forehead. "I realized I didn't ask, but you said you went to the doctor."

Hailey waved a hand in the air. "Just a cold and ear infections."

Landon narrowed his eyes wondering if she was minimizing it. Then again, he didn't know anything about kids being sick. "Sorry about that," he said.

"It's okay. They'll be fine."

"Landon! Come see what I built with Legos!" Carter yelled, taking Landon's hand and dragging him down the hall.

Landon laughed as they moved toward the boy's room. When Carter produced his creation, Landon put his hands to his face and dropped his mouth open. "Wow! Dude, that's so cool. Tell me about it." Landon dropped to his knees on the floor and listened as Carter explained every detail. When the boy was done, Landon gave him a high-five. "That's creative, buddy. You're one smart dude." Then he grabbed Carter with one arm and ruffled his hair with the other.

"Hey!" Carter yelled in protest.

"Oh, what? You don't want me to mess up your hair?" Landon ruffled it again, and Carter let out a combination of squeals and laughter. They dissolved into a wrestling match on the floor with both of them laughing.

"What's going on in here?" Charlotte appeared in the doorway to ask. She must have been trying to sound grown-up.

Landon reached over and tugged her braid. "Just a little fun."

Charlotte giggled.

"Kids, come eat dinner," Hailey called out.

"Uh-oh," Landon said, poking out his bottom lip. "The fun police said it's time to stop."

"Pizza!" Carter yelled, and all the kids ran down the hallway.

Landon took his time standing up from the floor. A brightly colored fabric being blown by the air vent caught his gaze, and he turned to look at the window. The curtain hung at a strange angle. He reached for the fabric and pulled it back, revealing the problem. The curtain rod had been pulled from the wall and hung by a loose screw. Hmm, Kyle would never have let something like that sit broken. Poor Hailey probably hadn't had time to fix it. Or didn't know where Kyle's tools were.

Landon knew. He could fix that up in about five minutes.

The loud voices of the kids drew him back to the kitchen and he walked that way. Taking in the room, he noticed a few other things that needed to be fixed, or at least some attention from someone taller than Hailey. The fan blades looked like they had an inch of dust on them. His mind went to Hailey's van, and he wondered if she was keeping up with the maintenance on it. That was something Kyle had always handled.

His mind reeled. How could he bring up those things to her? Should he even be the one to do that?

As he made his way into the kitchen, he caught Hailey's eye as she wiped her hands on a kitchen towel. "Do you want some pizza?" she asked. Her voice was kind, but her face said she was ready for him to leave.

"Nah, I'm good. I'll get out of your hair."

"It's alright, you bought it. There's plenty here."

Landon had never been one to say no to pizza. "Alright, just a slice, and then I'll go."

"Thanks again for today. I'm sorry that I needed to call you."

Landon shrugged. "I didn't mind. I probably needed to stop staring at my computer screen for a little bit anyway."

"Well, I'll try to plan better next time."

Landon furrowed his eyebrows at her. "How would you have planned better? You couldn't know there would be traffic. Was there any other time to take them to the doctor?"

"No, it was the only appointment."

"So it's not your fault. You did the best you could do. It's okay to need help sometimes."

Hailey shrugged. "Like I said, I appreciate it."

Landon took a bite of pizza and chewed it as he rolled her words over in his mind. Surely she needed help sometimes. "Do your parents help with the kids?"

"Sometimes," she said in a tone that wasn't convincing. "They're out of town this week."

"They're out of town a lot," Carter said around the pizza in his mouth. "We don't see them much."

"That's not true," Hailey said, rolling her eyes. "Kids exaggerate. I called Claire today, but she's sick. You were my last resort."

Landon reached for a napkin and wiped his hands and mouth. "I don't have to be. I'm happy to help. Especially on a day when I'm working from home. Let me know if there's anything else I can do." He wanted to ask about the curtain, and when was the last time she'd changed the oil in the minivan, but he stopped himself. "But I'll let you guys get on with your evening."

"Aww, we were just having fun," Carter said. "After dinner all we do is homework and laundry."

Landon grinned. "I've got my own version of homework tonight too, and plenty of laundry. Let's hang out again soon, okay, dude?" Landon reached out to fistbump him.

Carter lifted his hand and nodded. "Cool."

Landon waved to Charlotte and Ellie, and then looked up to Hailey.

He stopped, frozen in place as he caught her gaze. She smiled, but it didn't reach her eyes. She looked tired and worn. Was it just a bad day? Or was she like this all the time? He cleared his throat. "I'll see you again soon," he said, wondering as the words tumbled out if they were really true.

"Okay," she said. "Thanks, Landon."

"Sure, no problem," he said. He turned and walked out the door, pulling it shut behind him. He could still hear the kids' voices as he walked down the front stairs and to his car. The drive to his house wasn't long enough to process all of the thoughts swirling around his head. So instead of turning right toward his neighborhood, he turned left.

He didn't have a particular place to go, but driving in the silence helped him think. How many drives had he gone on with Kyle when one of them needed to figure something out? He remembered the last one. He hadn't known it then, but Kyle had an inclination.

"I need to ask you a favor," Kyle had said.

"Sure, anything." Landon had never had a brother, but Kyle was pretty close. He was sure there was nothing Kyle could ask that Landon wouldn't agree to.

"Hailey and I have been going through some legal paperwork. I know it's terrible to talk about, but we have to have things lined up, especially with the kids. So we've drawn up a will and everything."

"Dude, this is depressing," Landon said.

"I know, but it has to be done. Hailey has a list of all the accounts and financial documents. If something happens to me, they should be okay money-wise." Kyle had parked in a spot at the edge of the movie theater parking lot, and he turned to look at Landon with an intense stare. "If something happens to me, I need you to promise you'll take care of them. Hailey will try to be tough and act like she can handle it on her own, but I need to know that someone is there for her. You're my best friend. Promise me you'll make sure they're all right?"

Landon remembered how he had looked his friend in the eyes and promised him. Then he went home and told himself it would never happen. Kyle was smart and tough. He was working his way up in the company, and he was in great health. What could happen?

Then came the day he got the phone call.

No. It couldn't be true. This was all a mistake. Sure, maybe there had been an accident, but Kyle would make it. He was the strongest person Landon knew. He would fight.

Landon hadn't realized he had driven right to the spot where they'd had that conversation. It seemed like years ago and only yesterday at the same time.

In reality, Landon had let more than a year go by. A year where he failed at keeping his promise to his friend.

Walking into that house and seeing Hailey there with all the kids, he knew exactly what Kyle had meant. Hailey was putting up a front. Sure, maybe she could handle it, but she didn't have to do it alone.

Landon had made a promise to help, and it was time to make good on that promise.

4

Hailey sat at her desk Monday morning chugging down her second cup of coffee. She'd already completed what felt like a marathon before seven a.m. Carter had been up in the middle of the night saying he couldn't sleep, something he did often ever since Kyle's death. Hailey didn't know how to help him, other than to let him stay in her bed, which meant she slept practically none.

Carter was hard to get up in the morning after that, and the girls were in a bad mood. Ellie said she didn't want to go to school. Charlotte wanted to go, but she wanted to wear her pink shirt, the one that was at the bottom of the pile of dirty clothes.

Hailey sighed now, thinking about how she had yelled that they didn't have time, and they had to go. Pretty sure she wasn't winning any mom of the year awards today. If only she could keep up with the laundry, or if she had breakfast ready for them on time. No, no, she wouldn't let herself start thinking like that. Charlotte would survive without the shirt, and Hailey had to keep moving forward. She was doing the best she could. Wasn't she?

"Hailey?" Her boss' voice from his office behind her desk brought her back to the moment.

"Yes?"

"We have a meeting with the Charity Event Committee at ten."

"Yes, sir. I'll be ready." She might need another cup of coffee, though. Those meetings could last for two hours, and she would leave feeling like it could have been a one-paragraph email. Still, it was part of her job as an administrative assistant at the bank corporate office, and she would do it with a smile. Even if it was a fake smile.

"Do you have the list of donors?"

She nodded. "I'll print it out."

"Great. The event is going to be our biggest one yet. I've heard they got that comedian, Josiah McClain, to be the emcee."

"I heard that too. That should be exciting and bring in a lot of ticket sales."

Hailey pressed her lips together and lifted her coffee mug in front of her face to hide her yawn until her boss disappeared back into his office. No matter who the celebrity guest was, she still wasn't excited about the meeting.

"Hey, girl," Jackie from the office next to hers said as she stepped into the doorway. "How was your weekend?"

Hailey lifted her coffee mug as if toasting her friend. "Great. I spent a relaxing Saturday sitting by the pool, reading a book, and catching some rays."

Jackie raised her eyebrows. "Considering it's November, I'm guessing that's sarcasm."

Hailey smiled. "We had a good weekend. I decided one weekend of skipping chores wasn't going to kill anyone, so we actually had some nice time together." She almost said "family time," but that phrase never felt right to her anymore.

"I'm glad. You deserve a break, girl."

Hailey rolled her eyes. "I don't see that happening anytime soon. But I'll take some quality time with the kids over scrubbing toilets. Tell me about your weekend."

"Oh you know, scrubbing toilets."

"No hot date?"

Jackie crossed her arms in front of her chest and leaned against the door. "Fresh out of those too. If you know any eligible men, send them my way."

Hailey laughed. "I'll be sure to do that, but you know the only man in my life is six years old."

"Hmm, true. Maybe we need to find you an eligible man too."

Hailey froze. "No," she said firmly.

"Hailey," Jackie said gently. "I know you don't like to talk about it, but you might be ready one day. I hate to see you believe you'll be alone forever."

"I'm not alone. I have three kids to take care of."

"I know, but you know what I mean."

Hailey shook her head. "I don't have any plans to date. Kyle was it for me. When I met him, I knew I had found my one person. That kind of thing doesn't happen again."

"You're still young," Jackie said. "I just don't think you should write it off forever. You don't know what might happen. There could be such a thing as a second ever after."

Hailey held a hand up. "I'm not even thinking about that."

"Okay, okay," Jackie surrendered. "I'll leave you alone. Besides, I need to get back to my desk. Pretty sure I have fifty emails from the weekend. Why do people send work emails on Saturday?"

Hailey smiled. "Because they're behind, just like the rest of us."

Jackie pointed her index finger at Hailey. "Girl, you got that right. See you later."

"See ya," Hailey said, turning back to her own computer. She went to work answering emails and making a to-do list for the week.

The job was one she never expected to have. She'd spent a few years as a proud housewife to Kyle while he worked hard and made his way up the corporate ladder. She'd never minded that. Kyle worked a lot, but when he came home, he was fully present there. He was never too good to load a dishwasher or vacuum a floor, even if it was after the kids were in bed.

And he'd made sure they were taken care of. His life insurance policy was the only reason they survived the first few months after his death. But Hailey knew they couldn't live on it forever. She took care of bills and tucked away a comfortable amount in savings. Knowing there would be unexpected expenses, sports, piano lessons, and eventually college for the kids, she started looking for a job.

Hailey remembered the day she was hired as an

administrative assistant. She had gone home and cried. Partially because she was relieved to find a job, and partially because she would be working out of the house every day for the first time since Charlotte was born. There was nothing to be done about it, though, and she tried to keep a stiff upper lip as she left that first Monday morning.

Her cell phone rang, startling her out of her trip down memory lane. Glancing at the caller ID, she saw Landon's name. Surely it was a mistake, and he was calling her by accident. She pressed the button and quietly said, "Hello?"

"Hey, Hailey." Landon's voice sounded chipper.

"Oh hey, I thought maybe you were calling by mistake."

Landon chuckled. "Nope, it's on purpose." She thought she heard him sigh. "I'm sorry I've been away so long that you would think I didn't mean to call."

"Oh." Hailey wasn't sure what to say to that. "Um, it's okay. I know you're busy. You've got a lot going on."

"That's true. I let my job keep me busy, and I like it. But the truth is, I'm not as busy as you are."

Hailey's heart pounded against her ribs. What was he saying? She cleared her throat. "Everyone is busy."

"I'm not too busy to help you."

Hailey's hand flew to her mouth. No, she didn't need this. Landon had his own life. He might have lost his best friend, but he could go on as normal and have a life. Hailey didn't want to bring anyone else into her grief and struggle. Besides, Landon was the perfect bachelor. What did he know about helping with kids and taking care of a house? How could he help her? Still her mouth couldn't form the words that her brain was spinning around and around.

Landon must have thought that meant he should go on. "I want to help. You're doing a great job with the kids and everything, I just think that I could help take some of the load off of you. So what can I do?"

Hailey took a deep breath. "It's okay, Landon. You really don't have to do that. The kids and I are fine. We've gotten used to things the way they are."

"And that's great. Except that I took too long to offer to help. I should have been there from the beginning. I should have offered to stop by with dinner or to take the kids on a Saturday."

"That's not your responsibility," Hailey said.

Landon took a deep breath and sighed so loud it buzzed in her ear. "You don't understand. It is. I promised Kyle that if anything ever happened, I would help take care of his family. I've failed at that, and it's time I start making up for it."

Hailey felt the fresh tears in her eyes. She took a moment to compose herself. "That's nice of you, Landon, but I'm sorry. I can't let you do that. Kyle is gone, and there's nothing we can do about that. But you don't have to keep that promise." She wiped her eyes. "Thank you for the offer, but we'll be just fine. I have to go now. Goodbye."

She hung up before he could answer. No matter what he had promised to Kyle, Hailey didn't need help.

And she didn't need her husband's best friend around, reminding her of everything she'd lost.

5

T he next afternoon, Landon tapped his fingers on his desk in order from index finger to pinky and back again. Over and over the rhythm pounded in his fingers. His brain told him he needed to focus on work, but his thoughts were elsewhere.

With Hailey and the kids.

What was her life like? Going to work, taking care of kids, cleaning house, making meals. No one was supposed to do that on their own. Kids needed a mom and dad, and wives and husbands needed each other. Did Hailey have anyone to talk to? To confide in, and to say it's been a hard day? Or to share something great that the kids did?

Landon shook his head. Kyle was great at all of that. He couldn't count the times he called his friend, and Kyle was taking one of the kids for ice cream, buying flowers for Hailey, sweeping the back porch, or taking the garbage to the road.

The last thing he wanted was to take Kyle's place. No one could do that. But that didn't mean Hailey should do it all by herself. Kyle had said she would act like she didn't need help. Was that what she was doing? Just pretending like everything was fine.

He made up his mind right then and there that he wasn't asking for permission. He had made a promise, and unless Hailey pushed him out the door and locked him out, he was going to keep it. It was time to start showing up. Kyle had shown up for him plenty of times when he was the one being stubborn. Now he would return the favor.

With that decided, his mind—and his conscience—was finally clear for him to get back to work. The hours flew by as he dug into the project. He had always been able to focus laser sharp when he got in the zone. When he looked up, it was already inching close to five. Normally he would be settling in for a few more hours of work, but today he had somewhere to be.

He picked up his laptop and cord and slid them into his bag. He could always work at home later tonight.

In his car, he zipped to the interstate, hoping leaving a few minutes earlier would get him past the rush-hour traffic. It took longer than he wanted it to, but he still made good time.

Before six o'clock, he was standing on Hailey's doorstep knocking. He heard the kids running to the door, each of them yelling that they would be the ones to open it.

Just as the knob turned and opened slightly, he heard Hailey yell, "Don't open the door!"

Landon froze. Was he about to walk into a scene he

shouldn't see? What was happening that she was desperate for them not to open the door?

The door slammed back shut, and Landon stood waiting, unsure what to do, but only for a moment. Hailey opened the door and peeked out.

"Oh hey, Landon."

"Is everything alright?"

She furrowed her eyebrows. "Yeah, why?"

"Oh, I just heard you yell not to open the door, and I didn't know if something was happening in there."

Hailey opened the door wider and leaned against the frame. "It's just a rule that the kids aren't supposed to open the door when we don't know who it is. You never know what crazy people are knocking."

"Oh, right." He wanted to smack himself in the forehead. Of course it wasn't safe for kids to open the door to strangers. If he was going to help out around here, he definitely had a lot to learn. He cleared his throat and grinned as he held up his hands as if surrendering. "Just this crazy guy here."

Hailey let out a short laugh. "I think maybe you're safe."

Landon glanced past her and could see the kids peeking around to see him. "Hey, guys." He waved.

"Hey, Landon!" Carter yelled. Ellie and Charlotte hid behind their mom with shy smiles.

"Could I talk with your mom for a minute?"

"Are you staying for dinner?" Carter asked.

Landon glanced at Hailey and saw that uncertain look in her eyes. "Just let me talk with your mom, then we'll see what happens."

"Okay, I'm going to get my soccer ball." Carter took off running, and the girls followed his lead.

Hailey didn't move from her spot but crossed her arms in front of her. "What's up?"

Landon had tried to prepare the words to say, but now they seemed to disappear from his mind. He stuck his hands in his back pockets. "Listen, I know you said everything is fine here, and I'm sure it is. But that doesn't mean it can't be better. Kyle was a rockstar. I know he helped out around the house and with the kids, and even if you can do it by yourself, you were never meant to. Let me help, Hailey. Kyle was my friend, and I spent way too many hours over here with all of you to just walk away. I'm sorry it's taken me some time to realize that. I want to help out. What can I do? Bring dinner? Fold laundry? Pick up the kids from school? I'm sure you've got a lot on your plate. I'm here to let you hand some of it off. The kids know me, or they did before anyway. Let me hang out with them while you go grocery shopping or just take time to go drink a cup of coffee by yourself."

Hailey sighed. "I don't know."

"Come on, Hailey. You know me. I'm safe. Let me do this for you, and for Kyle."

She looked up at him then and uncrossed her arms as she took a deep breath. Her eyes were tired, but she looked almost ready to give in. "I don't want you to feel obligated."

"I don't. I want to do this. Just tell me what I can do."

She put her hand to her forehead. "We're about to eat dinner, but Carter has soccer practice tonight. You could take him to that."

Landon clapped his hands together. "Perfect. I can do soccer practice."

Hailey stepped back and opened the door. "Do you want to eat dinner? We're having spaghetti. I never understand the serving size of spaghetti noodles, so basically I have enough to feed a small army."

Landon laughed. "Great, with the kids and my appetite, we're basically a small army."

Hailey cracked a smile, which felt like a small victory. If he could take something off her plate, that would be great. If he could make her laugh again, that would be a miracle.

Something inside his heart beat out a funny rhythm at the thought of her smile. What if Hailey could be happy again? Kyle would want that, wouldn't he? Landon wasn't looking for anything more than to help her, but if helping could bring the life that seemed to have gone out of her, that would be the best thing he could hope for.

He stepped inside and closed the door behind him, stepping over shoes and backpacks in the doorway.

Carter came crashing through the room kicking a ball.

"No soccer in the house," Hailey called out.

"Sorry, Mom," Carter said sheepishly. He looked up at Landon and smiled. "Want to go outside and play soccer with me?"

"I think I'm going to help your mom get dinner on the table. But what about if I take you to soccer practice tonight?"

"Really?" Carter asked, his eyes growing wide.

"Yep. Your mom said I could." Landon felt like a little

kid who had gotten permission to hang out with his friend.

"Yes!" Carter jumped into the air. "That's awesome."

Landon smiled as the boy ran off to tell his sisters the news. How badly did Carter need a male role model in his life? He had his granddad, didn't he? Surely Landon wasn't the only one giving him attention. He told himself it was just because Carter thought he drove a cool car. Which he did, if he said so himself. He worked hard and rewarded himself with it when he'd been at the company for five years. It was great to be able to buy the nice things he wanted, but something about sharing them with someone else just hit him differently.

"Dinner in five minutes," Hailey called out.

Landon swiftly moved to the kitchen. "How can I help?" He practiced the question he planned to ask a lot.

Hailey bit her lip from where she stood, dishing food onto plates. "Um, here, you can take these to the table."

He grabbed the plastic plates from the counter and carried them.

Hailey pointed as she spoke. "The pink one is Charlotte's, it goes there. Ellie's is purple and goes beside her. Green is Carter's at the end of the table."

"Got it," Landon said, following her directions. "What color is your plate?" he asked with a twinkle in his eyes.

"White," she said. "But I'm the only one who gets a regular grown-up plate."

"Oh, I see." He tilted his head. "What about me?"

"I guess you can have a grown-up plate too. Unless you want a blue plastic one. All kid plates seem to come in either pink and purple or blue and green. With only one boy, we have extra boy colors."

"As much as I like blue, I think I'll take the bigger white plate."

"Wise choice." Hailey nodded.

As she filled glasses with milk and set them on the table, Landon took it upon himself to gather the kids. "Carter, Ellie, Charlotte, come to the table. It's time to eat."

The kids came to the table, wide-eyed. He guessed they weren't used to a booming male voice in the house. Hailey's voice was much softer and higher-pitched.

Each of the kids took their seats, and Landon watched as Hailey moved to the table. His stomach twisted as he looked at the available seats and wondered where to sit.

"You can sit here by me." Carter pointed to the empty seat on the side of the table. It wasn't the head of the table where Kyle had always sat, but it was next to Hailey. Landon decided to go with it.

"Thanks, bud."

"Let's pray before we start," Hailey said, folding her hands together and bowing her head.

Landon did the same and closed his eyes. He tried to listen as Hailey thanked God for the food, but his mind was busy with his own prayer.

He prayed for this family, that God would allow him to help them. And that He would protect his heart from the pain of missing his friend.

And from the sudden loneliness he felt sitting around this table with the little family he had missed so much.

6

H ailey checked her watch for the umpteenth time. Why couldn't she just relax? Carter was with Landon, and the soccer fields were ten minutes away at the most. Besides, practice wasn't even supposed to be over yet.

She sighed and looked around the living room. Normally on soccer nights, the girls had to be dragged to practice when they were tired and cranky. Hailey felt rushed to get them to practice, and then rushed to get them back home, showered, and in bed at a decent time. Too many times she had considered just pulling Carter out of soccer. But he loved it, and he remembered Kyle playing with him in the backyard and promising him he could play when he was six. Kyle had started at six, and that was the age he wanted Carter to start. So Hailey had signed him up, as promised.

Now the girls were already bathed and in bed looking at books quietly. Hailey took a deep breath, realizing that it had been much more relaxing. The girls had played together after dinner, and she had managed to clean up the kitchen and even pick up the living room while she waited for Carter to get home.

She hated to admit it, but having Landon take him really did help. Not that she would let herself get used to it. Landon could have a meeting next week, or decide he was too busy, or even have a date. She chuckled at that. In all the time she'd known Landon, he'd only been on a handful of dates. He said he wasn't interested, but people were always trying to set him up. He was good-natured enough to go and be polite, but she was pretty sure he'd never gone on a second date with any of the women.

Why was that? Sure, he was busy with his career, but was that all he really wanted? Kyle had always wanted the best of both worlds—career and family. Maybe that was more unique than she had realized. She frowned remembering that Kyle had been overlooked or turned down for promotions more than once. He always said he was fine with it, but she knew it was because he refused to stay late for those after-dinner meetings. And he'd turned down an offer to move once because the kids were settled in their school. Now it meant the world to her. All the promotions in history couldn't compare to having him home for dinner. They would never get that time back, and knowing now that his life had been cut short, she knew he had made the best decision when it mattered.

She heard the girls starting to talk in their room and decided it was time for bed. In their room, she stacked their books for them, sang a song, and whispered a prayer before turning out the lights.

"Goodnight, Mommy," Ellie said.

"Goodnight, sweetheart. I love you."

"I love you too, Mommy," both girls said together.

A smile hung on Hailey's lips as she made her way back to the living room. She sat down on the couch just in time to hear the door open and Carter yelling excitedly.

She stood up and made her way to the door, with her finger to her lips. "Shh, the girls are already in bed."

"Oh, sorry, Mom," Carter whispered loudly.

"How was practice?"

"It was great!"

Hailey lifted her eyes to Landon who was shutting the door. He grinned and gave her a thumbs-up.

"Landon coached us!"

Hailey's eyebrows shot up. "Oh?"

Landon shrugged. "The head coach wasn't there. I guess he was sick or something. Apparently the other volunteer dad had to be in charge, but he said he doesn't know much about soccer. He's usually there to wrangle the kids and tie shoes." He laughed. "I asked if I could help, and he said, 'Do you know anything about soccer?'"

Hailey laughed then too. "Did you tell him you made it to the state championships in high school all four years?"

Landon grinned and shook his head. "No, I just told him I played before, and he handed it off to me."

"Landon should coach all of our practices!" Carter said. "It was awesome. We did drills and ran and played a slimmage game."

Landon patted him on the shoulder. "Scrimmage, buddy."

"Oh, right. Whatever. Anyway, my team won by two points, and I scored a goal."

"That's great, buddy, I'm proud of you. Now it's time to run get a shower, so you can get to bed," Hailey said.

"Aww, man, do I have to?"

"Carter," Hailey's voice was firm. "I gave you an instruction."

"Yes, ma'am." He turned to go.

"Bye, little dude. I'll see you later," Landon said.

Carter ran back for a fist bump. "Bye. Will you take me to practice next week?"

"Absolutely."

"Awesome," Carter said before running down the hallway.

Hailey turned and took a seat on the couch, motioning for Landon to sit. "Well, it sounds like you were a hit."

Landon looked around before taking a seat in the arm chair, the farthest seat away from her. "I'm just glad I could help. It was fun. And it's time I put my soccer skills to some good use."

"Do you still play in the adult league?" Hailey asked.

He nodded. "Yep. We haven't started back yet, something about a scheduling conflict with the fields. But we'll be back at it soon."

"That's nice," Hailey said, tucking her feet under her. She racked her brain for something else to say. It had been too long since she'd talked with him by herself, and besides, he and Kyle usually went back and forth so fast, there wasn't room for her to get a word in.

Landon tapped his fingers on the arms of the chair as if he sensed the awkward silence too. "I guess I should let you get back to your evening." He stood.

Hailey did the same. "Actually, it's because of you

that I even had an evening. I would be rushing to get the kids bathed and in bed now." She cleared her throat. "Thank you, Landon. This really was helpful. And besides, if I had taken him to practice, it sounds like it wouldn't have been much of a practice anyway. I've watched a lot of soccer games, but I don't think I could go out there and coach with the girls hanging onto me the whole time."

Landon smiled. "I'm sure you would have handled it. From what I can tell, you've handled a lot on your own. I'm just glad you let me do this for you. And I meant what I said about taking Carter next week. It's the same time, right? I've already put it on my calendar."

Hailey stared at him in wonder. "Yep, same time." Did he really want to do this again?

He clapped his hands together. "Perfect. I'll plan on it. What can I do between now and then?"

"Nothing. This was plenty. Don't want you to wear yourself out."

Landon pressed his lips together as if he wanted to say something but stopped himself. "Alright then. I'll plan on this, for now. Have a good night, Hailey. Thanks for dinner."

She walked him to the door. "Bye, Landon."

He lifted a hand in a wave as he jogged down the stairs.

Hailey shut the door and watched him from the window. He climbed in his car and pulled out of the driveway. She watched until he was out of sight and whispered a prayer that he would make it home safely. It was only a few minutes away, but anything could happen.

As she crashed back onto the couch, she sat thinking about how the night had gone and what it meant to her.

Landon had always been a good friend to their family, and he just wanted to help. But she had to keep her guard up. He could change his mind at any point, and she would be alone once again.

Yes, she could let him help out some, but she wouldn't let herself depend on him. Her heart wasn't fully healed yet, and she couldn't risk depending on someone again.

7

L andon paced his office as he listened in to the conference call with an earpiece in. He tried sitting down but couldn't stay still. Every time he sat, he would stand back up and start pacing again. It must be the excitement from the night before. He had expected to just take Carter to practice and back home. He would feel good about having helped Hailey and call it a night.

But when he got out there on the field with the kids, it was like a switch flipped inside of him. Suddenly he was having fun. Carter talked non-stop the whole ride home, and Landon knew things had changed. Yes, he was glad it had helped Hailey, but it was like he was back in the position of fun friend, just like it was before.

Kyle had always wanted Carter to play soccer, just like the two of them did. Almost every time Landon was over at the house, they would make their way out to the yard to kick around the ball. How could he have forgotten that? Playing soccer with little kids wasn't really about winning championships or drills. Sure, that was part of it, but they just liked being out there having fun. Landon had missed having fun.

He tossed a ball back and forth in his hands as he listened to one of the upper-level managers talk about next year's projections.

Landon used to think that was fun, and it was still interesting, but today it couldn't hold his attention. He was thinking about when he could stop by the house again and be around the family. Did they still like to play board games on Friday nights? It was a standing tradition for a long time, and Landon had been more times than he could count. Or maybe they still planned their Saturday around the college football game sched-ule, so they could sit down and watch their favorite team.

For too long, he had thought it would be too painful to be around Hailey and the kids. Wouldn't that just remind him that Kyle wasn't there? But he had been wrong. He missed his friend, and it wasn't the same without him, but the kids were still there and Hailey...

Landon caught the ball in the air and stopped where he stood. What about Hailey? Would she let him come around more? Was it okay for him to spend time with her?

He shook his head. He wasn't spending time *with her*. He would be there with her and the kids. And they needed his help. Didn't they? There was nothing wrong with that. Besides, Kyle had asked him to. He was doing it for him.

The conference call ended, and Landon removed the earbud as he sank into his desk chair. He breathed a sigh of relief. Those calls got longer and longer it seemed. He only relaxed for a moment before his desk phone rang.

He saw the screen light up with his assistant's name and pressed the button. "Hey, Allison."

"Mr. Benton wants to see you in his office."

"Right now?" Landon asked.

"Yes," Allison said.

"Alright, I'm going." He stood and straightened his tie before slipping on his blazer that he took from a hook on the back of his door.

He passed his assistant's desk and held up his hands as if to ask how he looked.

She gave him a thumbs-up as she answered the phone.

Down the hallway, he pushed the button at the elevator and made his way up to the executive's floor.

Landon's own office was nice, but upstairs was truly the next level. Mr. Benton had two assistants who shared an office bigger than Landon's. They glanced up at him as he walked in.

One stood and asked him if he would like something to drink, while the other one picked up the phone and announced his arrival.

Landon held up a hand. "No thanks."

"He'll see you now."

He nodded at the two women before moving to the door. After one quick knock, he opened the door. "Afternoon, Mr. Benton."

"Richards, come in and have a seat." He looked past Landon out the door. "Miranda, can you bring us coffee, please?"

"Yes, sir," came the reply.

Landon took a seat and glanced out the large picture window behind Mr. Benton's desk. From up here, he had a great view of the city. Landon had always hoped one day to have a view of his own.

Mr. Benton waited while Miranda brought in a tray with coffee, cream and sugar, and two mugs. "Help yourself," he said to Landon.

Landon had meant it when he said he didn't need anything to drink, but now he reached for the carafe and filled his mug with coffee.

After Mr. Benton had done the same, he leaned back in his seat and dismissed Miranda. "Now, Richards, let's get down to it."

"Yes, sir." Landon wasn't sure what to expect, but he wasn't nervous. He was a good worker and did everything that was asked of him and then some. Surely whatever he had to say was a good thing.

"You've been busy around here lately."

Landon chuckled. "I try to be."

"Well, I've noticed. All of us have."

Landon knew he meant himself and all the vice presidents of the company. They always referred to themselves as "we," trying to communicate the message that they run the company together. "I appreciate that."

"You really stepped up with the One Source company project, especially when O'Neal was out sick the day of the meeting."

Landon nodded. "I want to be a team player. O'Neal did the best he could, but we didn't want him showing up less than his best. It's important we put our best foot forward in front of the clients."

"Yes, indeed. But you handled the meeting seamlessly. The clients were pleased, even though they were disappointed dealing with someone else when they'd expected O'Neal. Not a lot of people could have stepped in like that."

Landon's chest swelled with pride. "Thank you, sir. I did the best I could."

"That's exactly my point. You give it your best at everything you do. I like that. Some people show up and do fine. But you don't do fine, you do better than fine. That's what we want to see from our employees. And because of that, we want to give you a new opportunity."

Landon's heart pounded in anticipation of his next words.

"We'd like you to take over two of our accounts with Greenway Airlines. You'll be the account manager."

Landon couldn't help the wide smile that broke out across his face. "Thank you, I'd be honored."

"Wonderful. Harris has worked with the clients before, but these are new projects. He has taken on a heavier load with United Technologies, so he can't handle that now. He can bring you up to speed on what we've done with them before and make the introductions to their team. Then he'll hand it all over to you."

"Understood. I'm grateful for this opportunity. You won't be disappointed."

"I know I won't." Mr. Benton stood and shook hands with Landon.

"Miranda has the files for you. Stop by her desk on your way out. And, Richards?"

Landon looked up and raised his eyebrows.

"Good luck." The older man smiled as if he had just told a great joke.

Landon smiled back. "Thank you." He turned and left the office. He didn't have to stop at Miranda's desk, since she was already at the door waiting for him with a stack of manila file folders. He thanked her as he took them and continued walking.

He kept his composure all the way until he was inside the elevators and the doors closed. Then he jumped and pumped his fist into the air. He wanted to shout, but thought someone might hear him. This was just what he had been hoping for. The next step in his career and moving up in the company.

Back in his office, he set the files down on Allison's desk. "Guess what he wanted?" Landon said, putting his hands on his hips.

She smiled. "Apparently it wasn't to fire you."

"Nope, definitely not. He is making me account manager for Greenway Airlines."

She gasped. "No way! That's a big account."

"Yep. All those long hours and stepping in for the meeting for O'Neal are paying off."

Allison stood and they high-fived. "Way to go. You deserve it."

"Thanks. Congratulations to you too. I couldn't do it without you."

"You just remember that when it comes time for my Christmas bonus."

Landon laughed. "Don't worry. I won't." He glanced at his watch. "Oh, but before I forget. Will you put something on my calendar? For the foreseeable future, I need to leave by four forty-five on Thursdays."

Allison tilted her head and gave him a strange look. "You have a standing date?"

"That's right. With a six-year-old soccer team."

"You're coaching soccer?"

"Well, not exactly, but I might help out. I'm taking Hailey and Kyle's son Carter to his practices."

"Oh," Allison dropped her gaze and her eyes looked sad. "I understand. I'll put it on your calendar. If anyone asks why you can't meet, I'll say you're doing community service. That sounds nice."

"That's perfect, thanks." Landon picked up the folders and sauntered into his office. He plopped them on the desk and settled into his seat. Thursdays he could leave early, but tonight he would be staying late getting up to speed on these projects.

Oh man, he had planned to ask Hailey about Friday night board game night. He sighed, maybe he could do that next week. Or he could ask about the football game tomorrow. There would still be time for that, but he had work to do.

He had helped Hailey last night, and it was a satisfying feeling. Tonight, he could turn his focus back to the career he worked so hard for.

8

Hailey stood in the kitchen Saturday evening staring at the unbelievable sight in her living room. The Tennessee Volunteers were up by just three points in the last quarter of the game. That wasn't the part she had trouble believing. All her kids were crowded on the couch around Landon. He had called that morning and asked if they were going to watch the football game. Then just before game time, he showed up with wings and a tray of fruits and cheese. The wings were takeout, and the tray was one of the plastic kind from the grocery store, but he had done it all by himself.

Hailey pulled out chips and dip and made the kids peanut butter and jelly sandwiches while they all watched the game. Now the kids were on the edge of their seats, yelling and cheering at the TV.

She filled her glass with water before returning to her seat in the arm chair. The game was a nail-biter, but she couldn't drag her eyes away from the group on the couch. Surely Landon could be watching the game with other friends, or enjoying it in the quiet of his bachelor pad with the giant TV. She furrowed her eyebrows as she looked at him. Why did he look like he was having the time of his life right here?

Her attention was drawn back to the game as the team inched toward the goal line. With just ten seconds left in the game, they managed to score a touchdown and seal the victory.

The kids jumped and screamed and shook their tiny pom-poms in the air. Hailey laughed watching their antics. She let them carry on for several minutes before she looked at the clock. "Alright, it's time for everyone to get baths and showers. I let you stay up late enough, and we have church in the morning."

With groans of disappointment, the kids made their way down the hall.

Landon let out a long sigh as he sat back down on the couch. "Phew, that was fun."

Hailey looked over at him. "The kids certainly seemed to enjoy it. And by kids, I mean all of you."

He laughed. "I don't mind being a kid about a game like that. It's fun to watch when it's a close game."

"That is the best kind of game, isn't it? It's not too exciting to watch a one-sided score the whole time."

"I agree. I'll still watch it, and if it's my team, I'm glad we're winning. But yeah, I would rather finish the game exhausted from yelling and being surprised at every moment."

"The kids really got into it. I haven't seen them act like that about a game in a long time." She crossed her arms and stared at the floor. "Well, I haven't really sat with them during a game lately."

"Oh?" Landon propped his elbows on his knees and leaned forward. "Why not?"

She shrugged. "There's always something to be done. I just stay busy. I might catch part of the game, but I don't sit down and relax." She stood up. "Which is why I should be up now. The dishes and laundry aren't going to do themselves."

Landon stood too. "Which one can I do?"

Hailey gave him a funny look then busted out laughing. "Thanks, Landon, I needed that laugh. Just picturing you sorting through little kid socks and underwear is comical."

He planted his feet in front of her, and the look on his face told her he wasn't joking. "I'm serious. I'm here and I want to help. Which one do you want me to do, dishes or laundry?"

Hailey took a deep breath. Taking Carter to soccer had been helpful. Showing up for the game had felt a little bit like old times. Helping with household chores? That just felt personal. He would be in her space, doing work for her family. She couldn't let him do that, could she?

"Landon, it's awfully nice of you. And I know you want to help. Really, I can do this."

"I know you can. But you just said you don't sit down to watch a football game because there's too much to do. So if I help, that means you got to watch a football game, and you aren't behind because of it. Besides, what is the saying, "Two people can do two jobs faster than one person can"? He scrunched up his face.

Hailey chuckled. "I'm sure that's the exact saying. Fine, you can do the laundry. I'm warning you, though, it's kid laundry. That means a lot of small items." She pointed to a basket. "I fold them into piles for each child. The boy stuff is easy to tell, but if it's pink or purple, you have to check the size to see if it's Charlotte's or Ellie's."

Landon nodded. "I think I can handle it."

"I fold them standing at the kitchen table and put the piles in their spot. Then they have to put them away before they can eat breakfast."

"That's smart," Landon said, carrying the basket to the table.

Hailey shook her head as she moved to the sink. "You might have picked the wrong job. I didn't cook dinner, so there's not that many dishes."

"I'll do the dishes next time then."

His words made Hailey's heart skip a beat. Was he really planning to make this a regular thing? No, she couldn't think about that. Sure, he was here now, and he wanted to help. But it would fade at some point, or he would be too busy. Or maybe he would finally find someone he wanted to be with. Then she would be back to taking care of everything on her own. She cleared her throat and told herself to just enjoy it while it lasted.

"So how's everything at work?" she asked.

He glanced at her as if he was unsure about answering. "It's good."

"Oh come on, you can say more than that. I'm not a casual acquaintance who doesn't know anything about your job."

"Right. You know all about my job." He scratched his

head before picking up a pair of pink-striped pajamas and checking the tag. "Well, actually it's going really well. Mr. Benton called me into his office yesterday, and I'm now an account manager for one of our bigger clients."

Hailey smiled faintly. "That's great Landon, congratulations."

"Thanks. I've been hoping for it for a while now and putting in the time to prove myself."

She nodded. "I remember when Kyle got his first lead title on a project. He was so proud, and we both felt like that was really the start for him."

"I remember that too. The Deep South Grocers job."

"That's right. You were on the team. Weren't you?"

"Mmhmm. Kyle came straight to my office to tell me he got it and asked me to work with him. I had a full plate working for Harris' projects, but I would never miss the chance to work with Kyle. That's how we met, you know, my first day of work."

Hailey nodded. Of course she knew, but it felt nice to hear Landon talk about it. "Go on."

Landon glanced at her and met her gaze. Something passed between them as if he knew that she just wanted to hear it, even though she knew the story. They had a common bond in Kyle's stories.

"So I'm so excited for my first day, and I'm thinking I'm pretty awesome anyway. I had a brand new suit on and was carrying a briefcase my grandmother bought me for graduation. Pretty sure I thought I would be running the place by lunch."

Hailey lifted the back of her hand to her mouth to cover her laugh.

"I walk in, go straight to the desk, and tell the receptionist who I am." He rolled his eyes. "As if she was supposed to know all about the new guy sitting in the back cubical. She checks her computer, and I'm not even on the schedule. I start to panic. Maybe it was some cruel joke, and I didn't really get the job. Or I mixed up the day I was supposed to start. I'm just about to ask her to call someone when Kyle walks in the door." He paused and shook his head. "Man, he looked like everything I wanted to be. Professional, put together, confident. He stops and says hi to the receptionist, and she has this panicked look on her face. So he turns to me and introduces himself. I tell him I'm starting today, and he goes, 'Oh, right. I remember hearing that. Come with me, and we'll get you set up.'"

Hailey smiled picturing Kyle saying those words. "He always had a way of making everyone feel comfortable. And you're right, he must have sensed there was something wrong. He was so good at that."

"Yeah, he was. He took me back and introduced me to a dozen people and found where I was supposed to be. We were fast friends after that day. But I'll admit, I'm sure I was never his equal. I always looked up to him."

Hailey sniffed and looked at him. "He didn't see it that way."

"I know. That's what was so great about Kyle."

Hailey nodded. "He thought so highly of you. He was always saying you showed him something new, or that you were going to be the one moving up the ranks at work. And look, now you are."

Landon sighed as he set down the shirt he was folding and sank into a chair. "I miss him."

Hailey put the last dish in the dishwasher and shut it. As she dried her hands on a dishtowel, she walked to the table and sat opposite Landon. "Me too. All the time."

"How do you do it?" Landon asked.

"What?"

"All of it. Taking care of the kids, and the house, and being strong for them. How do you do it?"

Hailey propped her elbows on the table and dropped her chin into her hands. "Most of the time I feel like I'm failing. And I don't ever feel like I'm strong enough for them."

"You must be. I see them laughing and playing. They're taken care of. They're doing well in school. That's because of you, Hailey."

She shook her head. "I don't know." Could she really tell him the truth? The words she hadn't been able to say to anyone else. "I spend most days thinking that Kyle would be so disappointed."

"Hailey." Landon's eyes met hers, and his voice was tender. "Don't ever say that. Kyle would be so proud of you and the kids. You guys were all he ever talked about. I would be deep in a project at work and be asking him all kinds of questions, but, as soon as his watch beeped, he said sorry he had to go. He never wanted to be late to get home and see you. And he definitely wouldn't let a little pile of laundry and toys on the floor change that."

"I guess not. This was just never part of the plan."

"No one plans for this."

"I know. But I was a stay-at-home Mom. He told me

from the beginning he didn't want me to have to work when we had kids. I liked my job, so I stayed there until I gave birth to Charlotte. Then I thought maybe I would go back to some kind of job when they were in high school. I never expected to be working when they still needed me so much. I'm thankful I can be off in time to pick them up from school, but there's just no down time."

"I can't imagine. You're doing a great job, but I know it's hard. That's why I need you to let me help. I told you, I promised Kyle."

Hailey swiped at a single tear. "See? He was even trying to take care of me when he's gone."

"Would you expect any less?" Landon lowered his head, and his voice was soft.

"No, not really." Hailey took a deep breath and blew it out. "I was mad at him the night he died."

Landon furrowed his eyebrows in concern. "Really?"

"Yes. It wasn't that big of a fight, but I was upset that he had a dinner meeting. You're right that he didn't have them often, and he did the best he could to be home with us all the time. But he had that one, and it just irritated me because it had already been a long day. Then he called to tell me he would be late." She paused as the emotions washed over her. She sniffed. "I was mad about doing dinner and homework by myself that night, and I was harsh with him on the phone. As we hung up, I heard him say, 'I love you,' but one of the kids was climbing on something, and I just hung up without saying it back."

"Hailey, that's just one moment of all the years you had together. That phone call wasn't all your relationship was. And he knew you loved him. Trust me."

"But that was it. The last time I spoke to him, I was in a rush and didn't even finish the phone call. And I was upset. Then two police officers showed up on my doorstep."

Landon moved to the chair next to her and put a hand on her arm. "I can't imagine what that was like."

"It was terrible. I mean, of course, it was. How could it not be terrible for someone to tell you your husband died? But I had the girls in the bathtub, and Carter playing in his room waiting for his turn. I hadn't even cleaned up from dinner because I thought I would do it after the kids were in bed." She stared at the kitchen table, but in her mind, she could see it all so clearly. "Those dishes sat there for two days until my sister came over and washed them. I can't believe I was even able to get the girls out of the tub. I just lost it right there. Kyle was everything. The glue who held our family together. Sure, I took care of the house and the kids, but I didn't make the important decisions on my own, or fix the cars, or anything. How could I ever go on without him?"

"I remember when I got your text. I couldn't believe it. I had just walked in the door, and I literally fell over onto the couch. It just couldn't be true. At first I was sure it was a mistake. I started calling anyone I could think of that might know for sure. I didn't want to call you. I finally got a hold of Deacon, and he told me it was true. That there had been a car accident on the interstate and Kyle didn't make it. Until that moment I didn't let myself believe it. I think I hung up on him."

"I don't blame you. I wish I could have slammed the door in the officers' faces and pretend it wasn't real.

Telling the kids was the worst. Even then, I don't think they really understood. It took a few weeks for them to stop asking me when he was coming back."

Landon sighed and pulled his hand away.

Hailey looked at the spot where his hand had been on her arm and realized how comforting it had been. She couldn't explain why, but she wished he would put it back. "I didn't mean to tell you all that, but I'm glad I did. My family has been supportive, and friends too. No one understands, though. No one had Kyle in their life every single moment of every single day." She looked at Landon. "No one but you. The two of you were closer than anyone I know."

"We were. I never had a brother, and Kyle was like that. Except maybe closer because we didn't have the baggage of growing up together and fighting. I'll always miss him, but I'm thankful that I got to have him in my life."

She nodded. "That's a nice way to look at it. I'm sure he felt the same way about you."

"But, Hailey, you have to stop talking negatively about yourself. You're an incredible mom, and you're doing great with the situation you've had to walk through. I know you don't see yourself as the leader of the family, because Kyle did that so well, but you've stepped up and done what needed to be done. Don't ever say that he would be disappointed in you because that wasn't in his vocabulary."

Hailey looked up at him and held his gaze for a moment. "Thanks, Landon. I think I needed to hear that."

"I'm happy to tell you because it's true." He sighed.

"Well, I'm sorry that we are at a place where we have to talk about this, but I actually feel a little better. This grief has been hard, but it's comforting to know we aren't in it alone."

The words surprised Hailey, but it surprised her more that it was true. "You're right. I'm sorry you lost your best friend. We enjoyed having you here tonight. I never meant to shut you out. If I did, I'm sorry."

"Don't apologize. I kept my distance for too long. But I realized that it wasn't just Kyle I missed. Your family was a big part of my life, and I've missed that. I want to help, but I didn't know that I actually needed to be here for me too. I'll always miss Kyle, but you and the kids are here, and I don't want to miss you."

9

L andon sipped his coffee as he walked across the parking lot early Saturday morning. If someone had told him he would be attending a gymnastics meet that day, he would have laughed in their face.

But when Charlotte asked him if he would come watch her do her floor routine, he said yes before he could even think about it. Her little blue eyes were so sweet and innocent as she pleaded with him, that it was impossible to say anything else. Still, he was used to watching soccer games or basketball or football. He didn't know what to expect from little girls' gymnastics.

"Hey, Landon," Hailey's voice drew his attention the moment he walked through the gymnasium door. She waved him over to where she stood with Carter and Ellie near the entrance to the gym.

"Morning," he said cheerily. "How is everybody?"

Hailey smiled but blew out a big breath. "We're here, but it's a feat."

"You should be the one getting a medal. It's just me,

and I had to drag myself out of bed. Getting three kids up and ready before eight a.m. is incredible. You're amazing."

Hailey's cheeks flushed pink, and he realized he was paying her a compliment. It felt nice to say that about her. She was amazing, and he wanted to tell her that. His heart beat out a funny rhythm as he realized how true that was.

"Thanks," she said. "Charlotte's out there warming up. We have about twenty minutes before they start, so we should go get our seats."

"Perfect. Come on, guys," Landon held the door open and gave Carter a nudge. Ellie made her way beside him and slipped her hand in his. He held on tight to the little girl as they moved through the crowd of people. "Woah," he said as they found seats in the bleachers. "I had no idea this many people would be here."

Hailey smiled. "I think there's about a hundred gymnasts competing in this session. And that's just her level and age group. So multiply that by parents, grandparents, and siblings, and it's a lot of people."

"Cool. So I don't know much about this. Will you explain it to me as we go along?" Landon asked.

"I think you'll figure it out. I'll tell you when Charlotte's about to compete on each event. Just cheer for her when she's done, and you'll be just fine."

He gave her a thumbs-up. "That I can do." He looked over at Carter. "So do we get snacks at these things?"

Carter scrunched his face. "Mom brought fruit and water in her bag."

Landon cut his eyes to Hailey and she shrugged.

"That's awesome. You need healthy snacks to help you

grow and be strong, especially if you want to be an awesome soccer player."

Carter gave him a look that said he knew that was a line.

"Did you bring some for me? I love fruit and water."

Hailey pressed her lips together to stifle a laugh as she nodded. "Plenty for everyone." She mouthed, "Thank you," for only him to see.

Landon nodded in understanding. It was fun being the "cool guy" that the kids wanted to be like. If he could use that power for good, he definitely would. "So how long do these things last?"

Carter groaned. "Forever."

Hailey gave him a sympathetic look. "A few hours. You don't have to stay the whole time. Do you have any other plans today?"

As Landon watched her talk, he suddenly knew that if he did have plans, he would cancel them. His heart thudded in his chest. Where had that come from? Sure, he was glad to be there, and he was enjoying helping out, but that was about the kids, wasn't it? It wasn't about spending time with Hailey. So why did he feel like there was nowhere he would rather be? He cleared his throat to answer. "Nope, no plans. I just wondered if we would be done in time to go get some lunch."

Carter gasped. "Can we?" He looked to Hailey. "Please, Mama, can we go out to eat?"

Hailey blinked rapidly. "I don't know. We'll have to wait and see." She looked to Landon. "We don't really go out much. Three kids in a restaurant by myself is a lot to handle. They try to behave, but, honestly, sometimes it's just more enjoyable to eat at home."

"I understand. I could pick something up and bring it to the house. Or we could try it. You don't have to do it alone."

Just saying the words seem to ease her mind. Hailey smiled and nodded. "Sure, let's see what time we get out of here, but we can give it a try."

Landon caught her eye and grinned. He held her gaze for just a moment longer than he meant to. He'd never noticed just how deep brown they were. She held a seriousness there, and he wondered if she held a playful nature that not many people got to see. If only she could let go of the heavy burdens she carried to get back to living life.

That thought stayed with him as he watched the girls on the gym floor. Hailey pointed at Charlotte and explained each event. Before the competition was over, Landon had learned all about Olympic order and the complex scoring system for the gymnasts. When it was Charlotte's turn, the kids yelled her name over and over, wishing her luck. Hailey only let one cheer out, trying not to distract her. Landon held his applause until she was finished. Then with his booming voice, he called out, "Way to go, Charlotte!" She was a distance away at her event, but he was pretty sure he saw her turn and grin in his direction.

Carter fidgeted in his seat most of the meet. Hailey tried to keep him entertained, but there was only so much sitting a little boy could do.

"Want me to take him out to the hall and stretch our legs?" Landon asked.

"You don't mind?" Hailey asked.

"Not at all. Come on, Ellie, you come too." He reached for the little girl's hand. As he walked behind her on the bleacher, Landon put his hand on Hailey's shoulder and leaned down to speak close to her ear. "Just sit here and enjoy a few minutes to yourself. I won't say quiet, because it's not quiet, but take a breath. I've got this." He straightened as he pulled away from her, he hadn't realized how being that close to her would affect him. "Want me to bring you anything? Water? Coffee?"

Hailey spoke quietly, "No thanks. I'm fine."

"Okay, we'll be back in a little bit."

HAILEY COULDN'T HELP BUT WATCH LANDON WALK TO THE door with Carter bouncing up and down, and Ellie holding tight to his hand. When they were out of sight, she turned her head back to the meet, but her mind was somewhere else entirely. For a moment, she followed Landon's advice. She closed her eyes and breathed in and out. The echoes of the gymnasium seemed to fade a bit, but the only thought in her mind was the scent of Landon's cologne as he leaned close, and the sound of his voice so close to her ear.

Why did that make her stomach feel like a home for a thousand butterflies? He was just here to help with the kids, wasn't he? But wasn't he also trying to take care of her? She'd known Landon for a long time, longer than any of her other friends. And he'd spent more time with their family than others. In all that time, she'd never thought of him as a man.

Until this moment.

He was handsome, smart, and confident. She'd thought that before, but it had always been because she was thinking of who she could set him up with. A man like that needed to find someone to share his life. Her heart pounded a wild rhythm as a terrible thought washed over her. She would hate it if he found someone else now.

She snapped her eyes open and looked for Charlotte. If she could watch her daughter, she could push these thoughts away. Besides, she wasn't interested in Landon. That was completely ridiculous. She was only upset at the idea of him finding someone else because she liked having his help. Wasn't she?

Charlotte was about to compete on uneven bars, and Hailey clapped her hands together and yelled out her name. "Come on, Charlotte. You can do it!" Silently she told herself she could do it too. She could push away the silly thought of being anything more than friends with Landon. That's not what she wanted anyway. She'd been through enough loss. Sure, she appreciated Landon's help, and as long as he wanted to, she would let him. But she would have to work harder at keeping him at arm's length.

And at convincing her heart to stop racing when she saw him coming toward her with her kids happily walking at his side.

10

"I'm sitting by Landon," Carter called out as they walked toward the restaurant.

"No, I am!" Charlotte fired back.

"Both of you come and walk beside me," Hailey said firmly. "This is a parking lot."

Carter looked to Landon and moved toward him. "You better listen to your mom," Landon said.

Carter sighed as he walked to Hailey's side.

Landon pressed his lips together to keep from laughing at how dramatic they were, as if the world might end because they had to walk next to their mom. He reached the door first and held it open for Hailey and the kids to walk through. Hailey passed close to him, and he could smell her perfume. The teasing scent of light floral wafted towards him, and he caught himself closing his eyes to breathe it in. Just as quickly, he chided himself for his response. He couldn't be drawn to her. But he didn't remember her ever smelling like that before. They'd sat next to each other at the house last week, and he could swear he would remember that. He shook his head as he let the door go and walked in after them.

Hailey had already told the hostess how many were in their group, and the woman was gathering menus and crayons before she asked them to follow her.

At the table, Hailey settled the seating argument by telling them all where to sit. She made Carter and Charlotte sit next to each other, which left Ellie on one side, and as Landon slid into his chair, he realized that meant Hailey was next to him. A small feeling of joy flickered through him.

"Mom, I want corndogs," Carter said.

"Can I have grilled cheese?" Ellie asked.

"No, I'm not coming to a restaurant and spending seven dollars for you to eat grilled cheese," Hailey said. "You can have chicken fingers, a cheeseburger, or corndogs," Hailey said as she glanced over the menu.

"What am I allowed to have?" Landon asked, turning to look at her with sad puppy dog eyes.

She swatted at him. "Whatever you want."

"Can I have a grilled cheese?"

She pointed an index finger in his face. "No grilled cheese," she said. She locked eyes with him, and he watched as she held her serious face for just a second. Then she dissolved into laughter.

Landon started to laugh too. He grabbed at her finger in his face and pulled it away. "You said I could have whatever I wanted."

"Nope, I changed my mind. You have to eat some kind of actual protein."

"Aww man," he whined.

"Just for that, you have to eat a vegetable too," Hailey snapped.

"Fine, but then I'm getting dessert." Landon smiled at her, suddenly realizing he was still holding her hand in his. He pressed his lips together and let go. Turning his attention to his menu, he could still feel where her hand had been in his for a brief moment. "Now then, let's see here."

He cut his eyes to Hailey, and she looked as affected by it as he felt. "What are you going to have?"

She held up her menu to block her face from the kids and whispered, "Grilled cheese."

Landon's lips slowly curved up into a smile. She was playing with him. Why did that feel so natural and so right? And at the same time so impossibly wrong? He couldn't look away, and he didn't want to. Finally, she broke contact.

"Just kidding," she said. "I love their parmesan crusted chicken. I'll have that and the sweet potato."

"That sounds good. I think I'll have the same." He wasn't sure he could focus long enough to pick something else.

"Really?" Hailey put her hand to her chest in surprise. "You're not going to have a steak? I've never seen you not order a steak."

"Well, you don't always eat with me. I eat things besides steak."

"Alright, then. Like I said, you can have what you want."

Landon stared straight at the table. What did he want? His mind whirled. Why was he here? Was he really at a restaurant for lunch on a Saturday with a beautiful woman and her three children? Just the idea sounded crazy in his head. This was never part of the plan.

Landon was trying to process his thoughts when suddenly his lap felt cold and wet. He gasped as the sensation ran through him.

"Oh, Carter, no!" Hailey stood and moved quickly grabbing napkins and scooping ice into a cup.

"I'm sorry, Landon," Carter was saying.

Landon held his breath and couldn't utter a word as he looked at the now empty cup lying on the table.

Hailey waved down a waiter and asked for extra napkins. When she had them, she shoved them in Landon's hands. He still hadn't moved.

"I'm so, so sorry," she said. "Are you okay?" Now she leaned down to look him in the face which finally snapped him out of his shock.

"Um, yeah, it's okay. I'm okay. It's, um, just water, right?"

"Yep, just water. Well, and ice."

"Oh yeah, I'm sensing the ice." He began to blot at his wet pants, not sure it was going to do much good. He hadn't been this wet since the last time he went swimming.

"They usually give the kids cups with lids. I was just about to ask if they could change it out." She bit her lip. "Guess it was too late."

Landon tried to laugh it off. "These things happen. I mean, I guess they do." He'd actually never had an entire cup of water spilled in his lap at a restaurant, but he was pretty sure he wasn't the first person in the world to experience it.

Hailey grimaced. "I told you. We don't go out to eat very often. At least when they spill something at home, there's a change of clothes available."

Landon chuckled. "That would definitely help."

"Do you want to go? It's okay. I completely understand if you do."

Landon looked up from the futility of trying to dry his pants. Glancing around, he saw the looks on the kids' faces, sadness and disappointment. His eyes landed on Hailey, and he saw her concern, and maybe even fear, that he would want to leave. He smiled, pushing through the discomfort of the cold. "No, no, let's just eat. It's just a little cold. I'll survive it."

Hailey gave him a sympathetic look. Then she leaned over and whispered, "You earned your dessert."

He wanted to tell her thanks and stare into her eyes as she smiled. But Carter was talking and calling his name.

"Landon, Landon."

"Yeah, bud," he answered.

"Did you hear that the rodeo is coming to town?"

Landon scratched his head. "No, I didn't know about that. I don't keep up with rodeos much. Tell me about it." He propped his chin in his hand and listened intently as the boy told him about the events. He described the smelly cows and the funny clowns, and how one time they had eaten nachos. "That sounds like a lot of fun," Landon said.

"It's the best."

Hailey gave him a weak smile. "I don't know when the

rodeo is coming to town. He just always thinks it will be coming soon."

"Oh," Landon said, not really understanding.

"We only went once, and I can't believe he remembers it so well. But Kyle wanted to take us. It was a lot of fun. I'm glad he has that memory."

The name hit him like a ton of bricks. This was still Kyle's family. They had memories with their husband and their father. He could never step in and fill that spot. The waitress came then to take their orders. Landon turned all his attention to the food, and to keeping an eye on the kids' water glasses.

He had wanted to step in and help Hailey. And he knew that was the right thing to do. She could use an extra hand, and he was happy to be that.

But he had to remember that was all he was there for. He had to shut down his senses to the sweet smell of her perfume, and the way her eyes lit up when she laughed. Maybe they could be friends, but nothing more.

And maybe what he had needed was a douse of water after all.

11

Hailey chewed her fingernails as she watched the front walk from the window. How had the week flown by, and it was Thursday night again? All the days and hours seemed to run together and last forever all at once. She used to look forward to Thursday nights. "Friday-Eve" they would call it. And Friday, when everyone came home from school and work, it was officially the weekend. The best part of every week.

Weekends were for family time. Kyle worked so hard to provide for them. But when he came home Friday, he hung up his work hat and filled their home with love, laughter, and life.

For the past year, Hailey hadn't even looked forward to the weekend. It was more work, more activities, and more time for her to be alone.

Tonight, Landon was coming to take Carter to soccer practice. Carter was already running up and down the hall in his practice gear. She had been so relieved to have

Landon help with this, and Carter loved seeing him every week.

Now she stood watching nervously for him to arrive. Was she doing the right thing? Was Carter going to be disappointed one day when Landon decided not to come?

She knew he meant well, but things happened. Plans changed or problems came up. And he wasn't really committed to them. If he had a work emergency come up, then he couldn't say he had a family thing.

They weren't his family.

Even if he wanted to help, there had to be a limit to what he could do.

And what would happen if he just decided not to come around anymore? The only thing holding him here was a promise he made to his friend. How long was that really going to last?

She sighed as she saw his car pull into the driveway. She wished she could sort out her emotions. Part of her was just relieved he was there at all. Part of her worried about the future, and a tiny part of her that she tried to keep locked away was thrilled at the mere sight of him.

At the sound of the doorbell, she moved toward the door. Too late, Carter beat her to it.

"Landon!" Carter yelled as he opened the door.

"Hey, little dude, are you ready already?"

"Yep. Come on!" Carter said, running out the front door.

"Aren't you forgetting something?" Landon asked.

"What?" Carter stared at him as if nothing in the world mattered but getting in the car and going to soccer practice.

"A little thing called dinner?"

"Oh, right. I was so excited I forgot we didn't eat yet."

A beeping sound in the kitchen interrupted them.

"That's dinner," Hailey said.

Landon looked up at her for the first time. "Hi," he said.

Why did that greeting make her heart skip a beat? "Hey." She looked away from him and walked to the kitchen. "I made beef enchiladas. I thought it would be something easy that he could just scarf down and go."

Landon chuckled. "That sounds about right. I love enchiladas."

"Oh good," Hailey said. Had she known that? She had made the recipe plenty of times before. Did she remember him saying he liked them and, subconsciously, that's why she had made them tonight. She took a deep breath. No, she was overthinking this. She had made a quick, easy dinner for her family. Landon just happened to like the same food she made. There was nothing to it.

Just like there was nothing to Landon helping out and spending time with them. It didn't mean anything about her. It was just for the kids, and it was more about Kyle than it was about her.

"Hailey," Landon spoke her name from the other side of the counter, but from the sound of it, he had said it more than once.

"Yes, what? Sorry." Her words came out all in a rush.

"Is everything okay?"

"Sure, of course, why?"

"I just asked how your day was. You didn't seem to hear me."

"Oh, yeah. I'm just focused on getting dinner on the table. Sorry about that. I guess I was in my own little world. My day was fine. How about yours?"

Landon's forehead creased, and he tilted his head. "Are you sure?"

"Am I sure I want to know how your day was?"

"No, are you sure you're just busy? Is there something going on?" he asked.

Hailey stopped what she was doing and sighed as she placed her hands on the edge of the counter and faced him. "Charlotte wants to ask you something."

"Okay, what's wrong with that?"

"It's just kind of a big deal." Hailey bit her lip.

Landon sank onto the stool, put his hands on the counter, and leaned close. "Do you need to prepare me?"

"I guess so. You can think about it for about two minutes until she comes in here." Hailey kept her voice low. "There's a daddy daughter dance at school, and she wants you to go with her." She couldn't look up to see his face. It was too much. "A lot of girls go with someone besides their dad, because of different situations. I asked her if she wanted to go with Grandpa maybe, and she said she would rather go with you. But he can take her if you don't want to, really it's fine. I know you have a lot going on, and you really don't have to do this if…"

"Hailey," Landon interrupted her.

She looked up at him, her heart pounding like a bass drum, and found him grinning. "Yeah?"

"Why are you saying that? I can't believe she wants me to go. I'm honored, and, of course, I will take her."

There it was again, that feeling of relief mixed with

total fear. "Okay, but only if you're sure. It's just little girls dressing up. They play music, and there's some snacks. I don't think you even have to stay too long. A lot of her friends are going, so you might not even have to entertain her too much."

Landon reached across the counter and put his hand on her arm. "Don't worry. I'm happy to go. Just send me the date, and I'll put it on my calendar."

"It's Saturday night," Hailey said, putting her hand to her chest, desperate to quiet the sound of her heart.

"Oh, that's soon."

"I know. I'm sorry. She didn't say anything about it until now. I thought maybe she wouldn't want to go, without…" She stopped herself from saying his name.

"Without Kyle," Landon finished for her with a whisper.

"Yes."

He nodded in understanding. "That makes sense. I'm glad that she wants to go. And if she wants me to take her, I wouldn't miss it for the world."

Hailey nodded and forced a smile before she turned back to get plates from the cabinet. The kids ran in and started talking excitedly to Landon, giving her a minute to collect herself while she set the table.

Kyle would be happy that Landon was the one to take Charlotte to the dance, wouldn't he? And if something came up, Grandpa could just take her. It would be fine. She tried to convince herself to let it go and not worry.

As if on cue, Charlotte ran over to her. "Mom! Landon said he will go with me to the dance!"

"Yay, sweetie, that's wonderful. You two will have so much fun."

"We have to pick out my dress."

"Yes, we do, we'll work on that later. Right now, it's time to come eat."

Hailey listened to the kids chattering away, but she couldn't focus on the words. Landon seemed to be handling it, so she nodded and said, "Mmhmm," a few times. She tried to put a name to what she was feeling. She wasn't exactly sad, but she wasn't happy. She was somewhere in a weird middle, and inside she felt as if her world was tipped on its side.

When Kyle died, it was completely upside down. She knew how she felt every moment. Sad. Broken. Grief stricken.

What was it they said, time would heal? She didn't feel healed, but maybe she was starting to learn how to walk forward without being in complete sadness.

A quiet whisper in her soul said that was the beginning of healing.

With Landon handling the kids, she stood suddenly and excused herself to her room. She managed to hold it together until she got there. Closing the door, she put her hand against it and leaned her forehead on her hand.

Taking deep breaths in and out was a chore. The pain of loss often came in waves, but this was different.

As the tears slid down her cheeks, she realized what it was. It was still part of the loss. A part she never knew could be so terrible. She was sad that she had been able to be happy.

Over the last month, Landon had lightened her load.

He had taken Carter to practice, helped with the kids at the gymnastics meet, and folded laundry. But he had also made her laugh. She didn't remember when she had genuinely laughed.

She had been happy.

And she had been certain she wouldn't feel that way again.

Was it fair that she was living life and laughing with the kids, when Kyle couldn't do that?

Quiet sobs racked her body, and she shook trying to keep it all in. "God," she whispered against the door. "Help me. I don't understand the way I feel. I've been sad for a long time. Losing Kyle was the worst thing I've ever experienced, and I didn't think I would ever heal from it." She tried desperately to swallow past the lump in her throat. "I didn't even want to heal."

Something washed over her, and she felt the Holy Spirit impress on her, *The Lord never wanted you to feel that way.*

She remembered something she'd learned as a child at Vacation Bible School when they taught them the shortest verse in the Bible. "Jesus wept."

"Jesus wept," she repeated to herself. "He wept over Lazarus dying. He knew what it was like to lose someone. And Jesus left heaven and separated Himself from the Father when He came to earth. God, I know You know how I felt when I lost Kyle."

I never left you.

The words broke her, and she took a deep breath, trying to muffle the sobs. "I know You didn't. But I felt alone, and I didn't know how I would ever make it." She paused to take a breath. "And now…well, I don't even know the words. I feel mixed up and not sure what I want. I think it's because it feels strange to be happy." She sniffed, realizing that was the truth. "God, that sounds so sad. Kyle wouldn't want me to be miserable for the rest of my life. Kyle was all about living every day to the fullest. He made the most of his life, and I'm so glad he wasn't someone who put off living life and having fun until later." She wiped at her eyes and straightened up, making a decision. "God, thank You for this life You've given me. I have three beautiful children, and I had a wonderful husband who loved me and our kids so much. Help me to go on living. Help me to know how to live. Show me what I'm supposed to do. I haven't thought of much more than getting from one day to the next, but it's time I think about that. Not only for me, but for the kids. We need to have a life. You said You came to give us life, and life more abundant. I think I've been missing that. God, please help me. I love You, God, and even though it was hard for me to believe for a long time, I know You still have good things planned for me."

In her heart, she felt a peace that she'd known before but that had been missing for a long time. She smiled faintly. Maybe this was the new beginning that she needed. A piece of her heart that felt like it had been missing clicked back into place.

With a quick check of her face in the mirror, she saw that she looked just a little bit different.

For the first time in a long time, there was hope in her eyes.

12

L andon leaned against the wall as he watched Charlotte dancing and talking with her friends. She seemed to be having a great time, and she certainly didn't look as awkward as Landon felt.

He had thought it would be fun, and it was, but he hadn't thought about the fact that he wouldn't know anyone.

He didn't hang out with a lot of men with young kids, and anyone he knew from work didn't live in Twin Creeks. Plus, he felt like he wore a neon sign over his head that said, "Not a Dad."

Did people know that Charlotte's dad had died? Or would they think he was her dad? Their first incident happened when they arrived and stood in line for pictures.

"Come on, little lady," the photographer had said. "Step up here and stand next to your dad."

"Oh," Charlotte had said quietly. She glanced up at

him, as if she didn't want to hurt his feelings, but she wasn't sure what to say either.

He winked at her and said, "I'm happy to get a picture with my favorite ten-year-old girl."

She had giggled then, and they had smoothed over the moment.

Now he wondered how many times he would do that. Was he going to hang around enough to be mistaken for her dad more than once? Landon swallowed hard as his nerves rose. He put his hand to his chest to feel his heart pounding at the thought. Was he doing the right thing? Of course, he didn't want to hurt Charlotte or any of them. He said he would be there, and he planned to. But what if Hailey found someone else? Would he be able to step aside and let someone else be part of their lives? He shook his head wondering if that would all be confusing for the kids.

What if all of this was only a temporary thing?

Something deep inside him told him he didn't want it to be. What had started out as keeping a promise to his friend had turned into so much more. He was becoming part of this family, and he liked it. He liked it a lot.

"Landon!" Charlotte came running over to him. "Come and dance with me." She grabbed his hand and pulled him to the dance floor where fathers and daughters were paired up dancing together.

Landon grinned as he dramatically bowed to her and Charlotte giggled. Then he held out his hand, and she took it. They swayed, and he lifted her hand as she smiled and spun in circles.

He hoped the moment would stay with her forever,

and he knew he would never forget it. Because even if he wasn't her dad, he was exactly where he was supposed to be tonight.

An hour and a half later, after the last song had played, Landon drove Charlotte home. He reminded her to be quiet in case her siblings were asleep.

When they walked inside the house, he found that the kids weren't the only ones sleeping. He held his index finger up to his lips, and said, "Shh" when he saw Hailey on the couch.

But Charlotte paid no attention. "Mommy," she said excitedly. "Mommy, we're home."

"Oh," Hailey sat up and yawned. "Hey, sweetie. Did you have fun?"

"Yes! It was the best."

Hailey ran a hand through her hair as she looked up at Landon. "I'm so glad. Were your friends there?"

"Yes, Kim and Sarah and Lily and Annie were all there."

"That's great, I'm so glad. I want to hear all about it tomorrow. But it's late, so go get pajamas on and brush your teeth. Tell Landon thank you."

"She has," Landon said.

Charlotte stepped close to him and wrapped her arms around his waist. "Thank you for taking me."

"Of course. I wouldn't have missed it. I had a wonderful time. Goodnight."

"Goodnight," Charlotte said. "Mama, will you come tuck me in?"

"Yes, I will. Go on, I'll be in there in a few minutes."

Charlotte's dress swished and swayed as she moved

down the hallway. Landon watched her go, and then sat down next to Hailey on the couch.

"Sorry, I fell asleep," she said.

"No need to apologize. Everyone is taken care of. I'm sure you've had a long week."

"You're probably the one who's tired. Did you sit down at all tonight?"

Landon chuckled. "Not a bit. It was fun, though. She seems to have a good group of friends."

Hailey nodded. "They're sweet girls. I'm so glad she has friends. I've been worried about bullies in school. I'm sure it will be different when she gets to middle school, but right now I feel like she's in a good place with a good group."

"That can make a big difference." He looked at her and realized how close she was to him. "What did you and the other kids do tonight?"

"Oh, it was a big event."

"Really?"

"Mmhmm. I put them in pajamas early and let them have popcorn while we watched a movie. I started it early, and they went to bed when it was over."

"Well, that sounds just perfect."

Hailey covered a yawn. "It was nice to just be with them and relax."

"Maybe we could do it again next week?"

Hailey turned and looked him in the eyes. "Is that really what you want to do?"

"What? Movie night? Sure."

"Not just movie night," she said. "All of this." She gestured around the room. "You've done laundry, taken

Carter to practice and Charlotte to the dance, and had water spilled on your lap at a restaurant. Are you sure this is what you signed up for?"

"Why? Are you trying to get rid of me?" Landon shifted in his seat to face her directly.

She sighed. "No, I'm not. I like having you here. It's just that I don't want to be a burden, and I don't want you doing this just because you think you have to."

His heart soared to hear her say she wanted him there. "Hailey, I do want to be here. I haven't thought of you as a burden for one second. I've only been afraid I'm stepping across a boundary somewhere. I don't know where the line is."

"The line for what exactly?" She bit her lip as their eyes met.

He cleared his throat, sure she could hear his heart pounding. He thought about his words carefully, and then decided he couldn't say what he really wanted. "Like tonight, I had a good time with Charlotte, and she seemed to have fun. But what do I say when someone mistakes me for her dad? I don't want to make it worse by saying I'm not and reminding her of Kyle, but I don't want her to think I'm trying to take his place either."

"So what did you say?"

"I just said I was with my favorite ten-year-old girl."

"And how did she take that?"

He shrugged. "Fine, I guess."

"I've been having some of the same thoughts. But maybe the kids are the ones doing it right by not over-thinking it. Maybe we should stop worrying so much."

"Do you really mean that?"

Hailey took a deep breath and blew it out. "I do. I've been praying a lot about how I'm supposed to live life. I spent a long time thinking I was never going to be happy again, and I didn't want to have fun because it wasn't fair that Kyle wasn't here to have fun too. But that's not right. God is showing me that He doesn't want that for me. I'm trying to move forward because I still have a lot of years here, and my kids have their whole lives in front of them. I need to be open to the future, and what God has for me next."

Landon closed his eyes and took a breath before he opened them again. "I think that's exactly what He wants you to do. And that's what Kyle would want you to do too."

Hailey reached over and patted his arm. "That's enough serious talk for one night. Tell me more about the dance."

"Well, there was music and snacks, and I didn't know a single person besides Charlotte. Oh, also, she's got some serious moves."

Hailey laughed. "Yes, she does."

"Did she get that from you? Because Kyle is a lot of things, but I've never seen him dance."

Hailey shrugged. "Maybe. I mean, I might have been on the dance team in high school."

"Really?" Landon asked.

She nodded. "My last two years. Before that I was a gymnast."

"A gymnast? I had no idea. I guess that's why Charlotte likes it."

"Yep. It's fun for me to see her, but I also kind of hoped

she would pick something else. It's a fun sport, but I had a number of injuries and my body suffered from it. But she loves it, and it's nice that we can share that."

"She's definitely got the coordination and rhythm. She barely let me lead when we danced together."

"Oh really?" Hailey laughed. "So you did a couple's dance? I wasn't sure she knew how to do that."

"We muddled through."

"I wish I could have seen that."

Landon locked eyes with her and leaned forward. "I could show you," he said, his voice soft and low.

Hailey blinked rapidly and put her hand to her cheek. "Um, uh," she fumbled over the words. "How? Do you have a video?"

"No, not show you like that." He stood up and held out his hand. "I could show you like this."

Hailey looked up at him. "Oh, you don't have to do that."

"I know, but I want to."

Slowly, she stood to face him. He still held his hand out, waiting. She met his eyes and stood perfectly still for several seconds. He was sure she was going to laugh or turn and walk away, then slowly, she reached out and put her hand in his.

He closed his hand over hers and wrapped his other arm around her back as she stepped in close to him. He didn't care who was leading as they began to step and sway together. There was no music, but he felt the rhythm in his heart. There were no words, but he felt the connection pass between them.

Hailey dropped her eyes from his, as she leaned close

and put her head to his chest. Landon sighed contentedly. Everything about the moment felt perfect.

The few short minutes felt like hours of holding her in his arms, and Landon could have gone on forever, keeping her close and not worrying about anything else.

Hailey tipped her head back and looked at him, "Landon," she said quietly.

"Hailey," he responded with her name, and it felt good on his lips. He'd never said her name with quite so much meaning behind it, and he wanted to keep doing it.

She looked like she wanted to say something else, but she wasn't sure.

"Whatever it is, you can say it," he said.

Her cheeks flushed an adorable shade of pink. "Landon, I..." Her eyes were soft and dreamy, and Landon let his gaze drop to her lips. He took one breath before slowly lowering his head.

"Mama?"

Hailey's face went white, and she jumped away from him as if lightning had struck at her feet. "Huh? What? Are you okay?" Hailey stammered.

"Are you coming to tuck me in?" Charlotte asked, rubbing her eyes.

"Oh, yes, yes. I'm coming right now." She went to her daughter.

Landon let out the breath he didn't know he was holding and crashed onto the couch. He heard Hailey quietly speaking as they moved down the hall. "Landon was just showing me how you danced tonight."

He put his hand to his forehead. Had they upset Charlotte with what she'd seen? Did they look as close and comfortable as he felt? All the worry came crashing down on him again.

The only thing he knew was that holding Hailey in his arms was the most wonderful thing he'd ever felt, and he couldn't wait to do it again.

And for that he felt completely terrible.

13

H ailey sipped her coffee while clicking through her emails Monday morning, but her mind was elsewhere. Charlotte had talked about the dance all weekend. Hailey couldn't remember when her little girl had been so happy. Ellie said she couldn't wait until she was old enough to go to the dance.

But Hailey carried the memory of her own short dance. It was sweet and simple, but dancing with Landon made her feel strong and comfortable. When she leaned her head on his chest, she felt like she wasn't carrying the weight of the world on her own anymore.

"Hey there, sunshine." Jackie interrupted her thoughts.

Hailey blinked rapidly as she turned to face her. "Hey, how's it going?"

"Nothing with me, but something is definitely going on with you."

Hailey felt her cheeks flush and tried to hide her smile. "What are you talking about?"

Jackie pointed her index finger from Hailey's head to her toes. "Something has happened. You're all smiley and look like you're about to giggle like a junior high school girl."

Hailey waved a hand in the air. "No, I am not."

Jackie rolled her eyes. "It's not even nine o'clock on a Monday morning. No one smiles like that on Monday. She stepped in and leaned against Hailey's desk. "I'm not going anywhere until you tell me."

"It's nothing," Hailey said. "I just had a good weekend. Charlotte went to the daddy daughter dance, we watched football together, and it was just all so nice."

Jackie narrowed her eyes. "Did you take Charlotte to the dance?"

"No, Landon took her." She couldn't help the grin that spread.

"Aha!" Jackie shouted. "There is something going on."

Hailey held up a hand. "No, there's nothing going on. He's just helping out with the kids."

"And did he come over to watch the football game?"

"Yes, it's becoming a tradition."

"So he's just hanging out with the kids, and you're there, but nothing's going on, even though you have that goofy smile on your face on Monday morning?"

Hailey held a finger to her lips. "Keep it down. Yes, there's really nothing going on. Except that I really enjoy having him around. I don't know. I guess I just feel not quite so…" she let her words drift off.

"Lonely?" Jackie finished for her.

Hailey sighed. "Yeah, I guess so. Plus, he's great with

the kids. They think he's funny and entertaining and just the coolest thing ever."

"And what about you?"

Hailey looked away but knew she had to admit it. "I think he's pretty funny and entertaining. But it's more than that. I didn't want to open up to him, but we started talking. At first it was about Kyle. He was our common bond. And no one wants to talk to me about Kyle. Most people think it's too sad, or that it will upset me. Not Landon. He has so many great memories with him that we can talk about and laugh and share. It doesn't feel as painful because I know he misses him too. That led to talking about other things, and now I don't know. It's like when something happens, and you just want to tell somebody about it. Now that's Landon."

"That sounds like more than nothing."

Hailey shook her head. "It has to be nothing or maybe just friendship. He was there when I really needed someone, and I'm grateful. It's nice to have him in our lives. But I'm not ready for more, and the kids aren't either. They like having fun, cool Landon around, but it's not a relationship."

"But it could be one day?"

Hailey shook her head. "I'm not even thinking about that."

Jackie shrugged as she stood up. "Maybe you should."

Hailey watched her go and considered her words. No, she wasn't ready for that. Landon was good company, and she was grateful for everything he was doing, but she couldn't think about anything more. What would people think if she started dating him?

She shook her head and told herself to focus on her work.

Landon was a good friend, and maybe she even liked him a little. But that was all it could ever be.

Anything else was just impossible.

14

S aturday night, Landon knocked on the door for the second time and stood waiting. He furrowed his eyebrows and wondered if he should be worried. The kids always came running right away when he knocked, unless they were already opening the door before he got to it. Just when he reached for his phone in his back pocket to call Hailey, the door opened.

"Hey," Hailey said. "Sorry, it just took me a minute to get here."

"Is everything okay," he asked, stepping inside. Still no sign of the kids, and it was quieter than normal.

"Well, yeah, it's fine, but I'm sorry I didn't get a chance to text you."

His heart thudded in his chest. "What's wrong?"

"It's okay, but Carter isn't feeling well. I think he just has a little bug. He has a fever, so he's in bed. The girls have been begging to spend the night at my parents' house, and Mom just picked them up a few minutes ago."

"Oh," Landon said, stopping in his tracks. "So no kids?"

"Well, Carter is here, but I don't know if he feels like eating or watching the game."

"So, um," Landon rubbed the back of his head, uncertain of his next move.

"I, um, I made soup in the crockpot this afternoon. It's ready, but I didn't know if…" she shrugged as if she couldn't say the words.

"If I would stay without the kids?" Landon filled in.

She bit her lip. "Yeah, I guess. I was going to text you before you came, but I was getting the girls' stuff together and checking on Carter."

"Do you want me to leave?" he asked, silently hoping that she would say no.

"I just don't want you to be uncomfortable. But I don't want you to go hungry either."

Landon smiled. "Soup sounds great."

Hailey smiled as she let out a breath she seemed to have been holding. "Great. I'll fix us some bowls, if you want to find the game on the TV."

Landon's heart beat at a rhythm he hadn't known before as he made his way to the couch. Maybe he would eat and leave. Hailey would understand. Wouldn't she? He had some work to get caught up on. They could eat, and he could stay for the first quarter. Then make his excuses to leave. Carter probably needed her attention anyway.

"What do you want to drink?" Hailey interrupted his thoughts with the question.

He held up his drink. "I brought my own."

She shook her head. "You and that Diet Coke."

"Yeah, I know. I should give it up, but I don't want to. It keeps me going."

"I guess there are worse things."

"You mean like the four cups of coffee you drink every day?"

She swatted at him playfully. "I don't have four."

"How many do you have?"

"Two," she said.

He tilted his head and gave her the side eye.

"Okay, sometimes three, but it's still not four."

Landon laughed. It felt nice to tease her. "And I don't have four Diet Cokes every day, so see, I'm fine."

Hailey rolled her eyes at him as she walked to the kitchen and returned with two bowls of soup.

"What? You mean we can eat this on the couch? I thought there was a strict no drinks or foods that are liquid on the couch rule."

She shrugged. "It's for the kids, but since they aren't here, I can let it go this once."

He didn't need a reminder that the kids weren't there. It was pulsating the entire room. He had never heard it this quiet. He reached for the remote. "Guess I'll turn on the game." He found the channel and sat back in his seat. For a while, he managed to sip his bowl of soup and act like he was intensely interested in the commentators.

"Yeah," he agreed with one of the announcers, "That was definitely off-sides." He enjoyed watching the game, but right now it felt like a lot of work. How long could he sit there and avoid talking to the woman who felt so close and so faraway at once? He cut his eyes at her and noticed that, if he just reached his hand out, he could take her hand. What would that be like? If only he wasn't too scared to find out.

The game went to a commercial break, and he stood, picking up his empty bowl. "Are you done? Want me to take these to the kitchen?" He heard his voice and knew he was talking too fast.

Hailey nodded but gave him a strange look.

He placed the bowls in the sink and wondered what he should do now. It was barely ten minutes into the game. If he left now, it would be awkward. Even more awkward than it already was.

"Hey," Hailey said from the couch. "Are you okay?"

He brushed his hands off and stuck them in his pockets. "Yeah, sure."

Hailey stood and moved to the counter. "It's kind of quiet, isn't it?"

He took in a breath and blew it out. "Yeah, it feels strange."

She nodded. "I know. I'm not used to it."

"Do you really want to watch the game? I don't want to interrupt your quiet evening. Would you rather be alone to watch a movie or just sit in the quiet?"

Haley placed her hands on the counter and for a moment she stared down at them. When she looked up, he couldn't understand the emotion when her eyes met his. When she spoke, there was a quiver in her voice. "I don't ever want to be alone."

That was his undoing. Landon moved to the side of the counter and wrapped her in a hug. At first, she kept her hands balled up into fists against his chest. He didn't speak, or move, but slowly she released her fists and moved her hands to return his hug by wrapping her arms around his waist.

They stood there in the silence. Landon was afraid to breathe and break the moment. It felt right to have her in his arms, to comfort her and to help her. So why did he feel like he should run out the door and never come back? He pushed the thoughts aside and breathed in and out as they stood together. Finally, he spoke the only words he knew to say. "You're not alone, Hailey. I won't let you be alone."

Hailey sniffed, and he pulled back to look at her. Tears trailed down her cheek, and he lifted a finger to catch one.

"Hailey, I've seen you spill enough tears for a lifetime." He closed his eyes and took a breath before opening them again. "I don't want to be the cause of any of them. I wanted to be here to help you, but I don't want you to feel alone, and I don't want to cause you any pain. I'll go or stay, whatever will make you happy."

She seemed to consider this as she blinked and looked away from him. When she looked back, her answer was confident. "Stay."

As slowly as possible, he slid his hands down her arms until his hand found hers. He held firmly to one hand as they walked back to the couch and sat down together. And Landon didn't let go.

He turned his eyes to the game, but he couldn't process any of what was going on. Hailey was sitting next to him, and he held her hand in his. Nothing else mattered.

He turned to her. "Are you watching this?"

She grinned. "Not really."

Landon grabbed the remote and muted the TV before he turned to her. "Then let's just talk."

"Okay, what should we talk about?"

"Tell me something I don't know about you."

Hailey laughed. "What could you not know about me? I have three kids, and I'm an administrative assistant." She held up her free hand indicating the room. "I live here, and this is my life."

"Yeah, I know about you now. What about before? What were you like in high school?"

Hailey snorted. "You do not want to know about that."

"Sure, I do."

"Well, there's not much to tell."

"You said you were a gymnast."

She nodded. "Yeah, I was. That took up most of my time. If I wasn't at school, I was at the gym. If I wasn't at school or the gym, I was studying, doing homework, or prepping for a competition."

"Sounds like you were a really dedicated person."

Hailey tilted her head. "That's a nice way to look at it. Other people would have said I was a boring person."

"What's boring about working hard at a sport that you love?"

"Right? I enjoyed it. Yes, it took a lot of time and hard work, but it was my thing. I just didn't have a lot of time for fun outside of that."

"Did you have friends?"

"Yeah, a few friends at school. But they never understood why I was rushing off to practice, or that I couldn't hang out on Friday night because I had an early meet. And back in those days, we didn't have texting, so if I wasn't with them, we were out of touch."

He nodded. "I know what you mean. It's strange really

that teenagers now are in constant communication with each other."

"Exactly. I see how it's nice, but it can be a distraction from being where you are in the moment," Hailey said.

Landon didn't want to be distracted from this moment in the slightest bit.

"What about you?" Hailey asked. "I know you played soccer, but the rest of your high school career is a mystery."

"No, it's not." He laughed. "You've heard plenty of stories of my high school days."

"Well, maybe I want to hear some of them again."

"Which one? The one where I got detention for leading the walkout over no pizza on Fridays? Or when I got pulled over for driving with paper flying out of my truck windows?"

Hailey grinned. "That one."

Landon squeezed her hand. "Okay, so we were in a prank war with my group of friends. It wasn't really a back and forth war, like you got someone and they pranked you in revenge. It was more like when somebody pranked you, you just moved on to the next person who hadn't been pranked. Except I was usually the one coming up with ideas, so I pranked more than one person. Anyway, this group of girls pranked me pretty good. Three of them worked in the office at school for extra credit or community hours or something like that. They had this paper shredder and they shredded all kinds of paper. So instead of throwing it in the dumpster, they bagged it up and took it to their cars. It must have taken them a long time, but they built up a stash. One Friday night after a football game, they went to my house. I had a reputation for leaving my truck unlocked." He shrugged. "I didn't keep anything valuable in it. So they got in and poured that shredded paper from the floorboards to the top of the windows."

Hailey put her hand over her mouth to quiet her laughter.

"On Saturday morning, I had soccer practice, so I came out of the house, walked to my truck, and saw all the paper stuffed in there. I was running late, so I shoved out enough of it to get in my seat, cranked it up, and drove off."

Hailey couldn't hold her laughter anymore and she doubled over. "So you're just driving down the road with paper flying?"

Landon laughed and threw his arms in the air. "Yep. Everywhere. I had the windows open, and paper is just flying out in these little tiny pieces. Next thing I know, I hear a siren behind me, so I pull over. At first I thought he was going to write me a ticket for driving with an obstructed view or something."

"No?" Hailey asked.

"Nope. Littering."

Hailey. "That's the best. So you just had to pay the ticket?"

"That was only half of it. The officer knew my dad, so I had to pay the ticket. That afternoon, I had to don that lovely orange vest and sweep shreds of paper off the side of the road. Oh, and I was late to practice, of course, and I had to run twenty laps, one for every minute I was late."

"And did you learn your lesson?"

"Depends on what you mean by that. Did I ever drive my truck full of paper? No. Did I stop pulling pranks, absolutely not."

Hailey shook her head as her laughter died out. "I would expect nothing less."

Landon grinned. "What can I say? I am who I am." He grew quiet as he stared at their hands linked together on the couch. With a contented sigh, he said, "Isn't it weird to know somebody the way we do and still feel like we're just getting to know each other all over again?"

Hailey nodded. "It's nice, though. It feels comforting that we have a background and we're not starting from scratch, but there's also new things to learn."

"I agree," he said, holding her gaze for a long moment.

"Mom," came the sound of a tired voice from down the hall.

Hailey jumped up and moved to check on Carter.

Landon stared after her and rubbed his hands together. It had been a long time since he'd even been on a date with someone, and while this wasn't a date, he'd certainly never been interrupted on a date by a kid calling from the other room.

Knowing it was time, and that it was the wise decision, he stood and went to the kitchen. With only his and Hailey's bowls in the sink, there wasn't much to clean up. In two minutes, he had them washed and sitting on the drying rack when Hailey came walking back into the living room.

"You didn't have to do that," she said.

"It's no trouble. How's Carter?"

"He's fine," she said. "He doesn't feel like he has a fever.

I was afraid he was going to be sick again, but he actually asked if he could have some crackers and Gatorade."

"That's a good sign."

She nodded.

As much as he hated to, he spoke the words. "I think I need to go."

Hailey's disappointment showed in her eyes but nodded in agreement. "I had a good time tonight," she said.

"I did too." He reached for her hand again, feeling like it was the most normal thing in the world. "I'd like to spend more time with you. But I want to be careful."

"I do too. Honestly, I'm not sure where this is going." Hailey bit her lip.

He gave her hand a squeeze. "I don't either. But I'm sure that I want to find out."

Landon pulled her into his arms for a quick hug. If he let himself linger, it would be too hard to leave. "Goodnight, Hailey," he said as he turned and made his way out the door.

As he walked to his car, he prayed silently for wisdom and patience. Because this was one thing he knew needed careful thought and prayer.

And he was certain he didn't want to mess this up.

15

L andon drummed his fingers on his desk Thursday morning. He hadn't seen Hailey since Saturday night, and his insides tossed and tumbled every time he thought about it. They had texted a few times, but he had kept things casual.

He shoved his fingers through his hair as he scoffed at himself. "What are you doing? You should just call her." But as happy as he was walking out of her house Saturday, he was too terrified to push forward.

What if the kids noticed his smile when he saw her again? What if someone else saw him with her? His best friend's widow.

And worst of all, what would Kyle think?

Landon sighed as he stood and paced his office. Too much was riding on this. He couldn't start something with her if it wasn't going to work out. The kids could be hurt, or Hailey. And if they ended it, he would just be right back to breaking his promise to Kyle. Kyle. Hailey's late husband. Ugh. It was all too much to think about. As he wore a line in the carpet, he began to whisper to himself. "Maybe you won't end it. What would that mean? That we get married?" He stopped in his tracks as the words slipped past his lips. "What if we got married?" His mind swirled with all kinds of new thoughts. Life together with Hailey and the kids. Was he really ready to commit to that?

He made his way back to his desk and collapsed into his chair. Before he knew it, his talking to himself turned into a prayer. "God, I'm lost. Life was going along just like I thought it would. My career is great. I live in a nice town in a house that's perfect for me. Just me. I wasn't thinking about dating anyone, much less getting married. And I most definitely was not thinking about dating Hailey. It's weird, right?" He paused and waited, hoping an answer would come down from the sky. He didn't see hand-writing on the wall or hear a voice, but he knew something deep in his soul. "Maybe it's weird. Maybe people will think it's strange, but all I know is I want to be with her. With them. With a family."

He squeezed his eyes closed. "I never wanted to want a family again." Thoughts of his own childhood tried to resurface, but he shoved the past away. "God, I don't know if I can even do it. I don't know how."

Quietly in his spirit, he felt a whisper say, *I will be with you.*

Landon sighed. "Okay, God. I don't know how to do this. And the whole thing still makes me feel like I'm shaking on the inside. But if this is the plan You have for me, I'm all in. Just don't let me do anything stupid."

HAILEY'S STOMACH FLIPPED BETWEEN EXCITED BUTTERFLIES and a terrible knot. Maybe the butterflies were just getting their wings stuck together. When Landon called that afternoon, she had been thrilled to hear his voice. For days, she had been afraid Saturday was just one fleeting moment of something between them, and that he wasn't going to talk about it again.

At the same time, she felt guilty that she wanted to talk about it again. She wasn't supposed to want to be with Landon. She wasn't supposed to want to be with anyone after Kyle. Was she?

All afternoon she had prayed that God would show her what to do. And then she would repeat to herself, "His ways are not our ways." What if God had a plan for her life that she could never have imagined? She certainly never would have imagined spending time with Landon. But now that he was here, it just seemed to fit. He was so different from Kyle, but when he was around or when he called, and she heard his voice, she felt a comfort she hadn't known since losing Kyle. And maybe that's just what God had planned.

"Come on, kids," she called out from the kitchen. "Landon will be here any minute." She heard a crashing noise from Carter's room and waited. Since no one cried, she went on. The girls came rushing down the hallway.

"Mommy, does this look alright?" Ellie asked, twirling in her pink and purple dress.

"Yes, sweetie, it looks perfect."

"Where are we going to dinner?" Charlotte asked.

"Actually, I don't know. Landon said he made a reservation and wanted to take all of us somewhere special." There were the butterflies, bumping into each other again.

"I hope it's somewhere fancy," Ellie said, pressing her hands together under her chin.

Hailey chuckled. Did Landon know what he was getting himself into? What if he really was taking her and three kids to a fancy restaurant? She squeezed her eyes closed and told herself not to worry.

The knock on the door told her there wasn't any time for that anyway. The kids began yelling and running to the door, fighting over who would open it. Before they could decide, Hailey pushed past them and turned the knob.

Her gaze fell on Landon like she had never seen him before. A soft gasp escaped her lips when she saw the black suit and tie he wore, and her eyes trailed down to the flowers he held in his hands.

"Hi," he said softly, silencing the yells of the kids. He separated the flowers and pulled out a single rose. "This is for you," he said, handing it to Hailey. He smiled only for her when their eyes met. It was only for a moment, but to Hailey, it meant the whole world. He turned his attention to Charlotte and Ellie and handed one daisy to each of them. "These are for you."

The girls squealed in delight.

Landon reached into his pocket and pulled out a small box. "And this is for you," he said, handing it to Carter.

"A Lego set!" Carter shouted. "Can we build it now?"

Landon shook his head. "Not now, we're going to dinner. But later we can build it together."

Hailey felt warm all over at the way he said "together" to Carter. She took a full breath for what felt like the first time in a long time. Tonight was going to be wonderful.

Hailey reached up to tuck a stray piece of hair behind her ear. Looking down at her simple pink top and dark jeans, she wondered if she should change. "I wasn't sure what to wear."

Landon looked over at her and smiled. "I think you look just fine. But wear whatever you're comfortable in."

She nodded. The outfit would have been fine for a family dinner, or taking the kids to a fast food place. But this wasn't either of those things. What was it exactly? A date? No, not with three kids tagging along. Still, something in Landon's tone this afternoon had told her it was important, and now he showed up looking like that. Hmm. She could have stared at him all night standing in her doorway. No, she couldn't go to dinner in this outfit when he looked that good. "Give me just a minute," she said. Without waiting for a response, she turned and hurried to her room. Once in her closet, she wondered what she would pick that might be appropriate. Most of her closet was full of jeans and T-shirts. Or work attire. Nothing said "fancy date night." She bit her lip as she remembered something and pushed clothes aside until she reached the back of the closet.

There was one dress she had bought that she had never worn. It was a dress she wouldn't associate any memory with Kyle. About six months ago, she had been browsing online late at night when she couldn't sleep, and this dress came up on the screen. At the time, she couldn't imagine anything she would wear it to, but something told her one day she would have a happy event to dress up in it.

She pulled out the deep red dress and held it up in front of her as she looked in the mirror. The bodice was silky, and the long sleeves were sheer red fabric. The skirt fell just below her knees in flowing layers, and she felt certain if she was a little girl, she would be tempted to twirl around in it. Yes, this was a happy event, and it was time. She slipped it on and only glanced in the mirror. The dress fit well, and, when she caught a glimpse of herself, she saw something in her eyes she hadn't seen in a long time. Joy. Her smile grew as she realized that was exactly what she felt.

Pulling on a pair of shoes, she grabbed her purse and walked back to the living room.

"Wow, Mommy, you look like a fairy princess."

Hailey heard Ellie's words, but she kept her eyes on Landon. He looked up at her, and he put his hand to his chest.

She felt her cheeks flush as she lowered her eyes.

He stepped close to her and waited for her to look up. "Are you ready?"

She nodded. "Yes, I'm ready." In every way.

As they herded the kids out the door, she reached in her purse and pulled out the keys and handed them to Landon.

"Really? You want me to drive?" he asked.

She shrugged one shoulder. "I don't know where we're going."

"Good point." He winked at her. "I'll be careful."

"I know you will."

A few minutes later, they were loaded and heading to wherever Landon had planned. "You know, it's kind of nice," Hailey said.

"What's that?" Landon asked.

"Having someone else make the decision. I'm happy to do it, but making all the decisions is just a lot. What time do we leave? What do we eat for dinner? What should everyone wear?"

"I'm great at making decisions," Landon said.

"So are you going to tell me where we're going?"

"Nope. You'll find out soon. Why don't you just relax?"

Hailey couldn't remember the last time she had done that. Maybe she could give it a try. She settled back in the seat and took a deep breath. Watching out the window, she noticed they were driving away from Twin Creeks and towards the downtown area. Landon must be driving back the same direction he had just come from to get home from work. She was reminded for the millionth time that he didn't have to be doing this. He could be enjoying his own dinner out somewhere, or sitting at home relaxing on his couch in the quiet.

The kids were talking excitedly in the back when they pulled into the parking lot of an upscale restaurant. She'd never been there before, but Kyle had been to dinner with a client there once. The knot in her stomach returned. "Are you sure about this?" She tilted her head in the direction of the backseat. "Really sure?"

"Absolutely." Landon glanced in the mirror, as if he was checking to see if the kids were watching, before he reached over and gave her hand one quick squeeze. "I spoke to the manager, and they have a private dining room in the back. We can enjoy the time and the food, and we'll be in an area where the kids are free to move around and talk."

"Oh." Hailey's voice was barely a whisper. She never would have thought of that. What a creative idea. "Thank you," she said.

"You're welcome." Landon grinned at her. "I want tonight to be special."

She nodded. "It already is."

After they parked, the kids piled out in the midst of Hailey's reminders to be calm and respectful of other people since they were in a nice place.

As they were ushered into the backroom, the kids were surprisingly well-behaved. They seemed to sense that this was important and tiptoed through the restaurant, taking it all in.

"I looked over the menu. They have cheeseburgers the kids might like, and a shrimp macaroni and cheese. Or they said they can make some chicken fingers if we ask the waiter."

"That's great." Hailey looked over the menu, frantically searching the dishes.

Landon brushed his hand across her elbow behind the table. "And everything is on me tonight. Order whatever you want."

"Landon..." she began.

He held up a hand to interrupt her. "I want to do this. Please let me."

She sighed as she leaned back in her chair. "Okay.

Only if it's what you really want."

"Trust me, it is."

Hailey tried to pick something that sounded delicious but was still reasonable.

The kids were so well-behaved that she was shocked. They talked and were a little too loud, but they stayed in their seats and ate their food without complaint.

"Why did we come to such a fancy place?" Charlotte asked over dessert.

Hailey's heart pounded at double speed when Landon cleared his throat. If he had something important to say, he hadn't told her.

"Because," he began and flicked his eyes to Hailey. "Because you're such a special family, you deserve a special night out. And because I like spending time with you and wanted to treat you."

Charlotte smiled as she took another bite of her hot fudge sundae.

"We like spending time with you too," Carter spoke up.

"Yes," Hailey agreed. "We do."

"I'm glad," Landon said. "Because I'm planning to stick around for a while."

"It's almost like being a family again," Ellie said quietly.

Hailey's eyes stung with tears that formed quickly.

Landon must not have heard her because he asked what she said.

"It's almost like being a family again," Ellie repeated.

Hailey watched the shock and sadness that washed over Landon's face.

He reached out for Ellie's hand. "Sweetheart, you never stopped being a family. I know it's different without your daddy, but your mom and your sister and your brother are still here with you. You're still a family, and you're loved and taken care of."

Ellie gave him a faint smile. "And now we have you too."

"That's right. You have me too. And I'm not going anywhere."

Hailey tried to swallow but felt like an elephant had sat on her chest. The words were too painful. Of course, he didn't think he was going anywhere, but he couldn't make that promise. Kyle thought he would always be with them too, but the future is never certain.

"I know I can't promise nothing bad will ever happen," Landon said, as if he read her mind. "But I promise I'll do my best to be here." His eyes met hers, and a silent promise passed between them.

In that moment, Hailey felt it in her soul that he meant the words he said, and that he cared about her and the kids more than she could know.

16

Hailey gripped Carter and Ellie's hands as they moved across the parking lot. "Charlotte, stay close to me, there are a lot of cars."

"Yes, ma'am," Charlotte said, following behind. "Mama, have we been here before?"

Hailey sucked in a breath, and the knot that had been in her stomach all morning rolled around. "Yes, sweetie, a few years ago. We came once when you were a baby, but you probably don't remember. Then we came once to watch Landon play."

"I think I remember that. Daddy was with us, right?"

"Yes, he was." Hailey swallowed as they stepped up from the parking lot onto the grass of the soccer field. Yes, Kyle had been with them. Now she was here with all three kids by herself to watch Landon play soccer. She was excited to see him, but her emotions were too mixed up to pick just one. How many people would she see today that would remember her from Kyle's days playing on the team? It had been a while, but lots of the guys were the same. Landon had said so.

Hailey wanted to shake herself. Just thinking of Kyle and Landon's names in back to back sentences was too much. Instead, she forced a smile. She was happy to be here, after all, and the kids would have fun. If she could just focus on that for the next few hours, maybe she would be okay.

"Hailey?" A female voice called out.

"Yes," she responded before she turned to see who it was. "Oh, hey, Ally."

"Hey!" Ally responded. "I haven't seen you out here in a long time." She turned and looked at the kids. "Hi, guys, how are you?"

"Hey, Mrs. Ally!" Charlotte moved forward to hug her favorite Sunday School teacher.

Ally smiled as she hugged the girl back. "I'm so excited to see you. Are you here to watch the game?"

"Yes, we came to watch Landon play!" Charlotte announced proudly.

Hailey felt her cheeks flush bright red, even though Ally kept her attention on Charlotte.

"Really? That's great. I'm here to watch Mr. Jackson. He plays on the same team as Mr. Landon," Ally said of her husband. She stood and straightened to speak to Hailey. "Julie is here too. She's watching Sarah. I just ran to the car for her blanket. It's a little chillier than I thought it would be. It's so hard to keep up with all the stuff kids need to go somewhere." Ally laughed.

Hailey nodded. "Oh yes, it is when they're little. It gets

a little easier when they get older and don't require so much every trip."

"I'm glad to hear that. I'm always afraid I'm going to forget something. The back of my car is loaded down with everything I might need, just in case. I don't know how you do it with three. I feel like I'm still figuring out one and don't know how I will handle two."

Hailey's eyes dropped as Ally rubbed her round belly. "Oh, congratulations! I didn't realize."

Ally beamed. "Thank you. We're very excited. And Jackson is thrilled we're having a boy!'

"Oh, how wonderful." Hailey loosened her grip on the kids as they all started walking again. Ally must be at least six or seven months pregnant. How had Hailey missed that? They had been close friends before. Kyle, Jackson, and Landon had all played on the soccer team together, and they'd been in Sunday school class with them for years. Hailey hadn't managed to get herself to Sunday School for a long time, but was she really so out of touch that she'd missed Ally's pregnancy announcement?

Charlotte and Ellie chatted with Ally as they moved forward while Hailey was lost in her own thoughts. How many meals had Ally and Julie brought to her in the months after Kyle's death? She couldn't say for sure, but it was more than once. And Ally had been the one to send her text messages and ask how she was and tell her she was praying for her. Hailey swallowed, realizing she had started ignoring the invitations to go to lunch or get a coffee. She certainly hadn't had time for the girls' nights they used to do. Now it was plain to her that she had put distance between them and cut herself off from her friends. She should have been there to hear her friend's good news and ask if she was having morning sickness or needed someone to watch the baby so she could nap.

Hailey watched Ally talking to her girls and made a decision. God was pushing her back into life. Landon was giving her the time and space to find joy again, and her friends needed to be part of that. She wasn't sure how to go about it, but she wanted to be in their lives again. Whatever that looked like in this new season.

As they neared the sideline, Hailey looked over to the team warming up on the field. She knew the moment Landon saw her. He had been kicking the ball with Jackson, but he stopped and immediately jogged to the side.

"Hey!" he called out. "You made it."

Hailey smiled. "We did, although there were a few moments I wasn't sure we would."

Landon put his hand on his hips and tilted his head to the side. "Any water spilling accidents this morning?"

"I only wish it was water. It was my entire mug of coffee. On Carter's outfit and the kitchen floor."

"Ooo," Landon grimaced. "Did the mug survive?"

Hailey shook her head. "Nope. Total loss."

"Oh no, I'm sorry."

"It's okay. It wasn't a special one. But it took ten minutes to clean everything up."

"And you're still early. I will never cease to be amazed." He met Hailey's eyes and winked at her.

She dropped her gaze, wondering if anyone else caught the exchange. "Well, we're here. So I guess you better play amazing today."

Landon chuckled. "No pressure, huh?"

"Nah. We'll still like you, even if you're terrible at soccer."

Landon glanced at the kids who were busy setting up their chairs to sit in. He took one step closer before he lowered his voice to say, "I like you, too."

Hailey didn't drop her eyes this time, but held his gaze for just a moment as her heart fluttered at an unbelievable pace. She pressed her lips together as she grinned. "Go on," she said. "Get to work."

He smiled at her before he jogged back to his position.

Hailey sighed inwardly as she turned her attention to the kids. "Okay, everybody got your seat?"

"Yep. I'm hungry," Carter said.

Hailey laughed. "You're always hungry. But we just ate breakfast thirty minutes ago. You can wait a little while."

She moved behind them where Ally was sitting with her sister Julie and their kids. Hailey took a deep breath as she approached them. "Hey."

"Hey, Hailey," Julie stood and gave her a hug. "How are you?"

"Good," Hailey said. "I've missed you girls."

"We've missed you too. I'm so glad to see you here. You guys should come every weekend. Most of our Sunday School class is here, and several other friends from church. It's a party every Saturday." Julie bit her lip as if she wasn't sure she should say what was on her mind.

Hailey understood and reached out to put her hand on Julie's arm. "I know, I haven't been around much. It's hard to call it our Sunday School class when I haven't been in at least a year. But maybe it's time I come back."

A smile spread wide across Julie's face. "We would love that so much. It's not the same without you."

"Thank you. It's been too long, and I think it took this time for me to realize I need that in my life."

"We're here whenever you need us. Anytime."

Hailey knew that she meant it. "Thank you. Can I sit here with you?"

"Of course. We've got plenty of room."

Hailey settled into her chair next to Julie, with Ally on the other side. She kept an eye on the kids as she chatted with the two women. In some ways, it was like no time had passed, and they fell into familiar conversation.

When the game started, Carter cheered the loudest as they watched the players move the ball back and forth down the field.

Hailey laughed every time he said, "Get it, Landon!" Even though someone else had the ball and Landon was nowhere near it.

How obvious was it to everyone that her kids adored Landon? And more importantly, was it obvious that she was starting to feel the same way?

17

"Richards," his boss' voice came over the phone Friday afternoon.

"Yes, sir."

"I need you to do something."

Landon grabbed a pen and the pad of paper on his desk, ready to take notes. "Yes, sir." He mentally ran through his clients and projects and wondered what was coming.

"I need you to go to the symphony."

Landon dropped his pen and tilted his head, furrowing his eyebrows. "Sir?"

"The firm sponsors the symphony. And we have a block of tickets. Some of the senior account managers were going to attend, but they're all tied up with other matters. We can't let the seats go empty. It would look bad on the firm," Mr. Benton said.

"Of course," Landon responded.

"We don't want them to think we just throw them

some money to look good and we don't care about the arts."

"Absolutely not," Landon said, even though he was pretty sure that was the truth.

"So will you go and represent us? Take some friends if you want, or dig up a date."

"Yes, sir. When is it?"

"Tonight."

"Oh," Landon's hand flew to his forehead as he glanced at the clock and saw that it was already three o'clock.

"My secretary has the tickets. Just stop by and get them. And take yourself to dinner on the firm."

"Yes, sir." Landon heard the phone click and dropped the receiver back into its cradle. He stared at his desk for only a moment before he grabbed his cell phone. There was only one person he wanted to take to the symphony.

"Hey," Hailey's voice sounded so sweet over the phone.

"Hey, I need you to get a babysitter for tonight."

"What?" Hailey's tone went from sweet to confused.

"I have to go to the symphony tonight to represent the firm. I have tickets, and I want to take you. So I need you to get a babysitter. Do you think you can do that?"

"Um…" Hailey's voice trailed off, and Landon could just see her biting her lip.

"We can go to dinner before. I'm sorry it's last minute. I literally just found out. It will be fun."

"Yeah, it sounds nice. I just, I'm not not sure about the kids. They've already picked out a movie they want to watch tonight."

"Well, they can do that. Could your parents come? Or

your sister? I'll order pizza, and then they can watch the movie."

"Yeah, I guess that would work. Let me see. But they might have plans."

Landon could hear the defeat in her voice. "I know you don't like changing plans at the last minute. I'm really sorry. I would have said no, if I could. Pizza and a movie sound great to me. But I have to do this." He paused and took a breath. "I would really like it if you could go with me."

He heard Hailey let out a breath on the other end of the line. "Okay. I'll see what I can do."

"Perfect. I'll be waiting to hear from you."

The next thirty minutes of work were excruciating. When Hailey finally texted and said her sister was coming over, Landon couldn't sit anymore. He clapped his hands together as he stood and gathered his things. His boss would understand that he needed to leave a little early to prepare for the unexpected evening, but Landon knew it would feel nothing like work.

Just after five o'clock, he knocked on Hailey's door. It immediately opened, but it wasn't Hailey.

"Hey," her sister Claire said. "I just walked in the door. Come on in."

"Thanks," Landon said. He cleared his throat, suddenly feeling awkward that Claire knew he was taking Hailey out for the evening.

"This is great, you know," Claire said, giving him a knowing look. "Hailey needs to get out more, and she could use a break."

Landon nodded. "I think so too."

"And it's good that it's with you," Claire said. "Just in case you wondered."

He felt like she had caught him, and he felt the color rush to his cheeks and chest. "Um, thanks."

"Hey," Hailey said, coming to the door. "Thanks for coming." She hugged Claire.

"Yeah, thanks, Claire, for doing this on short notice. Sorry I didn't find out until today," Landon said.

"No problem," Claire waved a hand in the air. "Deacon is at a conference this weekend. All I was going to do was veg out and watch a movie anyway."

"I hope the kids behave. They can watch a movie, and then go to bed," Hailey said.

"No worries. I can handle this," Claire assured her.

Landon checked his watch. "The pizza should be here any minute. I paid for it over the phone, so you just need to sign for it."

"Perfect. I love pizza. I promise, I got this. You two should just go before the kids come out and beg you to stay."

Landon chuckled, but only then did he allow himself to look at Hailey. "Wow," he said before he could stop himself. "You look amazing." She wore a navy dress that fell to just below her knees. Her high-heeled shoes made her taller than normal, and he could look her directly in the eyes.

"Thanks," she said, brushing off the comment. "Claire's right. Let's go before Carter finds out you're here."

He didn't say a word as he followed her out the door.

"Have fun!" Claire called out behind them.

Landon wouldn't even have to try. He knew he was about to have the time of his life.

The drive to the restaurant was filled with conversation from the day. Hailey told him about Carter's near injury on the playground when a kid dared him to jump from the monkey bars, and about Charlotte's grade on her spelling test, and about Ellie's disappointment in her afternoon snack. Landon relished it. He couldn't explain it, but it was so nice to hear about the ordinary parts of their life. And more than that, to know that now he was a part of it too.

"What are your plans this weekend?" Landon asked as they were seated at the table.

"Oh, you know, our usual excitement," Hailey answered.

"So, a trip to Paris? Broadway shows? Shopping?"

Hailey giggled. "Is that what you think we do?"

Landon couldn't help it. He reached out and took her hand in his. "No, but I think anything with you and the kids would be an exciting weekend that would rival trips around the world or expensive shows."

Hailey pressed her lips together and put her other hand to her chest. "Do you really think that?"

"Of course I do. And even if your weekend includes mopping floors and cleaning out expired food from the fridge, I want to be there."

"You're in luck then because that's exactly what's on my list."

"Great, what time should I be there?"

"Landon, be serious for a minute." Hailey paused and blinked as if she was carefully weighing her next words.

"Is this really what you want for your life? You are still young and single, and you're free to do whatever you want. I just don't want you to make a decision now that you regret later."

He rubbed his thumb over her fingers. "How could I ever regret spending time with you? Hailey, you are sweet and kind, and you're an amazing woman. I see the way you care about people in your life, and it makes me want to be one of those people."

"But are you really sure? Think about six months from now or more. Is this what you want?"

Landon sighed. "Honestly, Hailey, if you had asked me that six months ago, I would have had a different answer. All I cared about was my career, and I didn't want anything to tie me down or keep me from it. Then everything changed. You and the kids have shown me what it was like to be part of a family. A real family. I've never had that before, and I think I would be the luckiest man in the world to be part of it."

Hailey furrowed her eyebrows. "You didn't grow up with a family?"

Landon leaned back and pulled his hand from her as if recoiling in pain.

"I'm sorry. Did I say something I shouldn't have? I just don't know a lot about your family growing up."

Landon stared at the table. "It's okay. I don't talk about it much. Kyle knew, but I guess he felt it was my personal business." He folded his arms across his chest. "When I was a little kid, I thought I had a good family. My mom stayed at home with me and was there when I left in the morning and when I got off the bus. She did the best she could, but she was on her own most of the time. My dad traveled *all* the time. It started out as a few days here and there. Then we would see him on the weekends, and sometimes he would be gone for a couple of weeks. Then he would come home and stay for a month without leaving. During those times, he was an awesome dad. He took us to baseball games, concerts, the park, all kinds of places. When he was home, it was all fun dad all the time. Then I remember hearing him and my mom arguing at night when I was in bed. She would say he came in to have fun and leave again, and she was the one who was raising me and keeping the rules on her own."

Hailey reached out and put her hand on his arm. "That must have been hard on her and on you."

He shrugged. "I guess I was used to it. My mom had a lot to do, but I thought my dad supported us since she didn't have to work. So maybe it wasn't so bad. I was too young to understand." He swallowed hard to push down the emotion, so he could get the words out. "Then when I was fourteen, he was leaving on a trip one day, and he forgot his phone. My mom found it in the bedroom. When she picked it up and looked at the message on the screen, that's when she found out. The text was from another woman, and it said, "Can't wait for you to be home tonight.""

Hailey furrowed her eyebrows in confusion. She looked the same way he had felt when his mom showed him the message.

"After some digging and confronting my dad, she found out the whole truth. He had another family in the other town."

Hailey's hand flew to her mouth as she gasped. "Landon," she whispered quietly. "No."

He nodded. The fresh pain stung his heart all over again, and he waited to be able to breathe. Finally, he was ready to continue. "He had been with her for years. They have two kids, younger than me."

"Oh my goodness. I'm so sorry. I can't even imagine what that was like."

"It's all a blur now. I think I've suppressed a lot of my memories at that time. I don't remember much about that school year. I almost got kicked off the soccer team because I missed so many practices. But when my coach found out what happened, he let me stay, and he assigned my friends to pick me up and bring me to practice. That's the only thing that kept me going."

"So what happened with your mom?"

"She told him to take his stuff and never come back."

"Did the other woman know about you?"

He shook his head. "She found out when my mom called to tell her my dad left his phone. He had them both believing when he was with the other family that he was traveling for work. She screamed on the phone. I'm sure she was upset, but she decided to let him stay with her anyway. I guess it's because she still had little kids and didn't want to raise them on her own. Who knows? Maybe he just convinced her she was the one he loved. I've only seen my dad a handful of times since then."

"I'm so sorry, Landon."

He finally looked up at her again. "Thank you. Like I said, I don't like to talk about it. After that, I decided I would work hard and focus on my job. I figured it was better to just be on my own. I did my best to take care of my mom, but after I graduated from high school, she moved away. She said she didn't want to be reminded of the life she had with him."

Hailey sighed. "Didn't she realize she also had a life here with you?"

Landon shrugged. "I think it just hurt too much. She met a man on a single's cruise when I was in college and moved to South Carolina to marry him."

"Do you still see her?"

He nodded. "Usually at Christmas, and maybe one other time during the year. We talk on the phone at least once a week. She's happy with him, and I just hope he never hurts her."

"Seems like it will be okay, if they've been together this long." Hailey's tone was hopeful.

"She had been with my dad since their senior year of college. Married after that, had me three years later, and he met the other woman when I was eight. I don't think there's a time limit on walking out."

Hailey sniffed. "I understand. I know it's not the same thing, but I thought that Kyle would be with me forever. I took for granted that he would be there when the kids were graduating from high school and getting married. No, he didn't choose to leave, and I'm not saying it's the same thing. But I understand that life doesn't always go the way we think it will." She reached out and put her hand on his arm. "I'm so sorry he hurt you. People do things that don't make sense, and it just isn't fair. That must have been so hard on you at an age when a father is so important."

"I think that was the hardest thing. I decided then and there that I could make it without him because we already had. Then when I got older, I knew I never wanted to be that vulnerable to someone again. I decided I didn't want to get married or have a family; it would just be too hard."

Hailey pulled her hand back from him. "And now?"

Landon gave her a slight grin. "I feel like I've been given a family I don't deserve. Kyle was my best friend and a wonderful father. It's really not fair that he isn't here to see his kids grow up. I made a promise to him that I would be there for all of you, and I want to keep that promise. Now that I'm here, doing life with you and the kids, it feels like I don't deserve it. That makes me want to work harder for it and hope that somehow I can be half the man he was."

Hailey stared at the table for several moments as if she was thinking hard about her next words. "Landon," she finally said. "I don't want you to compare yourself to him. I know that's easy to do because you knew him. You saw how he was as a husband and a father. You're not the same man he was, but that's not a bad thing. You're you, and you don't have to compete with him."

Landon blew out a big breath. "I'm not sure about that. He's the only standard of a good man that I know."

"That's not true at all. God is the standard for a good father. He is the only one who never makes mistakes. Kyle made mistakes. I made mistakes. We all do. But God is always there to lead and direct us. If you focus on Him, instead of an earthly man, you'll be headed in the right direction."

18

Hailey lay in bed as the sun streamed in through the window Saturday morning. Claire must have let the kids stay up late watching a movie and playing board games because she hadn't heard a peep from them yet.

She was the one who couldn't sleep. Not with thoughts of Landon running around her mind.

How was this happening? She wouldn't have believed it in a million years if someone had told her that she would be considering a relationship with Landon, but here they were.

When he dropped her off last night, they held hands as they walked to the front door. They made it to the top of the steps, and he stopped and looked her in the eyes. "I had a great time tonight, Hailey. I love that we can just talk, and I feel like you hear everything I say. There's a connection between us that I've never had with anyone else."

She nodded slightly. "I feel that too."

He took her in his arms and she laid her head against his chest. They stood like that for a few moments in silence, and she breathed in his nearness. When he pulled back, he lifted her chin with his finger. His eyes dropped down to her lips and back up. Just when she thought he was going to lean in, he sighed. "Hailey, I want to do this right. I don't know what the rules are here, but I want to take it slow and be absolutely sure about the next move."

She nodded and swallowed. "Me too."

He hugged her again and then let her go as he stepped back. "Goodnight, Hailey. I can't wait to see you again."

His words had stayed with her all night, and she played them over again in her mind now. She couldn't wait to see him either.

But it wouldn't be today. He had already told her he had to go into the office today and prepare for a presentation on Monday. No, today it would be her and the kids. A smile played across her face as she realized that sounded wonderful. Too many Saturdays she had spent tired, exhausted, and worried. Only surviving from breakfast to bedtime had been her mantra for too long. Now she was sure she had the energy to make it through the day with the kids. They could have fun and laugh.

"God," she whispered. "Thank You. Thank You for never leaving me, even when I thought I was alone. I never thought I would make it without Kyle, but the truth is, You were the one seeing me through all along." Tears stung at her eyes. "Lord, I don't know all the next steps. Landon was not something I expected, and everyday I wonder if this is the right thing or if something terrible is about to happen. Help me to trust You and follow You in every step. Guide us and show us what You have for us. And help us to be patient."

"Mom," came a gentle voice from outside the door.

"Amen," Hailey said with a laugh. "Yes, come in."

The door swung open, and both of the girls came running into the room. They squealed and giggled as they jumped onto the bed.

Hailey laughed with them as she hugged them and kissed their cheeks. "Good morning, sweet girls. How did you sleep?"

Charlotte yawned. "Good. I could have slept longer though."

"Well, you didn't have to get up. You could have slept."

"I wanted to see you."

Hailey snuggled her oldest up next to her. "I'm glad. I wanted to see you too. Did you have fun with Aunt Claire?"

"Yes!" Ellie shouted. "She let us have chocolate chips in our popcorn."

"She did?" Hailey feigned shock. "She's just super fun, isn't she?"

"Mmhmm. And we made a fort with blankets in the living room and laid under it while we watched a movie."

"That sounds great," Hailey said.

"Did you see our fort?" Charlotte asked.

Hailey shook her head. "No, Aunt Claire must have cleaned it up for you."

"Oh yeah, she said she was the fairy godmother who cleaned up after we went to bed."

Hailey laughed. "She would make a great fairy godmother."

"Yeah, but it's only fun for some of the time. We like having our real mother here."

"Even if you have to clean up after yourself?" Hailey asked.

Both girls bobbed their heads up and down in agreement.

"I'm happy to hear it. So what do you want to do today?"

Charlotte furrowed her eyebrows in an adorable way. "What do you mean?"

"It's Saturday. What do you want to do?"

"Don't you usually tell us what to do?"

Hailey bit her lip. Maybe she did. "I do if we have something we have to do, but today there's nothing on the agenda. No gymnastics meets, or soccer games, or schedules. How about we have a fun day? You can pick something, and if it's reasonable and not too expensive, I promise I will say yes."

"Really?" Charlotte and Ellie asked together.

"Yes, really."

"Really, what?" Carter walked into the room rubbing his eyes and crashed on the end of the bed.

"Mommy says we're having a fun day, and we can pick what we want to do!" Charlotte shouted.

"Wow," Carter said.

"But choose wisely," Hailey said. "There are three of you, and, if you each pick one thing, that could take up the whole day."

The kids took on a serious look that made Hailey giggle.

"Why don't you get dressed, and then turn on a

cartoon in the living room while I get a shower. That will give you some time to decide, and then we'll get going on our day of fun."

They all jumped up and ran from the room, talking excitedly about the day and possible ideas. Hailey's heart soared to hear them. For too long they had all lived under a cloud of darkness, and today felt like a breath of fresh air.

Hailey hummed to herself as she let the hot water run over her in the shower and then took her time getting dressed and applying her makeup. The kids must have agreed on a show to watch for once because she heard them laughing happily instead of arguing. Yes, today certainly was going to be a good day.

When she made it to the living room, the kids jumped off the couch and began talking at once. Hailey laughed and held up her hands. "Okay, okay, I can't hear you. One at a time. Ellie, you go first."

Charlotte and Carter made a face, but quieted down.

"I want to go see a movie!" Ellie shouted.

"Oh, that sounds fun," Hailey said. "We'll look on the website and see if there's something playing we can go see. Okay, Carter you next."

"I want to go to the arcade!"

"That's another great idea. I think we can manage that one. Charlotte, what about you?"

"Mine is kind of two parts."

Hailey tapped her chin. "Well, tell them to me, and I'll decide if we can do it."

"I want to go to the mall and buy outfits for Easter and go to lunch at Lorenzo's."

Hailey's heart twisted a bit as Charlotte mentioned Kyle's favorite Italian lunch place. "That seems reasonable, and if everybody agrees about lunch, I think we can do both of those."

"Yay!" All the kids shouted together.

That night, Hailey collapsed into bed feeling happier than she could remember being in a long time. They had spent an hour at the arcade before going to the mall and lunch. Then they found a matinee showing of a cartoon movie that turned out to be hilarious and heartwarming. Instead of going home, she took the kids to play at the park until it was almost dark, and they picked up cheeseburgers for dinner on the way home. They had played and laughed all day, and she knew it was a day they would all remember.

As she fell into bed, she texted Landon about their adventures. The only thing that made her happier than spending the whole day having fun with her kids was the words he texted her in response.

I wish I had been there too.

19

After his presentation Monday morning, Landon sat rocking back and forth in his desk chair. The presentation had gone even better than expected, and the clients had seemed very pleased.

Mr. Benton had sat in the back corner for the entire meeting without saying a word. Landon wasn't sure whether to be worried or happy. He could be sitting in and waiting to congratulate him, but he was also known for showing up in someone's office with a list of critiques. Either way, he expected to hear some kind of feedback.

For the next little bit, he tried to focus on another project. He would get some notes from the client in a day or so and would be able to make changes and updates to the project from this morning. Until then, he was free to start on something else.

After lunch, he returned to his office and found an email from Mr. Benton's assistant. Just as he expected, he wanted to see Landon in his office that afternoon. Landon hit reply and let Miranda know he would be there in ten minutes.

He closed his eyes and folded his hands. "God, I never know what to expect from these conversations. I know I've done my best, and I want to leave the rest in Your hands. I pray that whatever You have for me, You would be the one leading me as I go into this. Amen." A sense of peace washed over him as he stood and made his way down the hall.

Miranda was on the phone but waved him through to Mr. Benton's office. Landon tugged on his tie before he opened the door and walked in.

"Richards," Mr. Benton's voice boomed. "Thanks for coming by."

Landon smiled, but chuckled on the inside. As if he had any choice when he was summoned to the office? "Yes, sir. Thank you for coming to the presentation this morning. Always nice to have your support."

Mr. Benton pointed at him. "That's exactly what I want to talk to you about."

Landon took a seat and braced himself. His boss had been smiling during the meeting, but everyone knew he could put on a good face in front of a client and tear you to shreds later.

Mr. Benton clapped his hands together. "That presentation was genius. The clients were eating right out of your hands. You could have sold them on anything you said."

Landon breathed a little easier. "Thank you, sir. I tried my best to research well and offer them marketing solutions for their particular needs."

"And that's exactly what you did. That kind of client care is exactly what we want. It's obvious you have your focus and effort in all the right places. I'm happy to see you so committed to your job."

Landon nodded, even as something inside of him shifted. "Yes, sir."

"Now, we have a new client starting out in a new market. I want you to take the meeting and make sure we land this deal."

"Of course, who's the client?"

"Hoffman Hotels and Suites."

Landon blinked rapidly and leaned back in his chair. "Aren't they based…" but Mr. Benton interrupted before he could finish.

"In Dallas, Texas."

Landon's insides started to churn. "You want me to take a meeting in Dallas?"

"Sure do."

"And then handle the project from here?" That wasn't how they usually did things, but Landon wanted to hope.

Mr. Benton folded his hands on the desk. "For now, yes. We'll see how it goes. We have a good team in place in Dallas. But I know this company, and I think you're the one to meet with the higher-ups."

Landon nodded, still feeling uncertain. "Of course. Happy to do it. When is the meeting?"

"Thursday."

"This Thursday?" Landon's head jerked back, and his voice went up a notch.

"Yes, exactly. Miranda can arrange your flight,

Wednesday morning, if possible. I expect you'll need to stay late tonight to get up to speed on the company."

"Yes, sir. Will do."

"Alrighty then. I won't keep you. Miranda will send over the file, and I'll let the team know you'll be there to handle the meeting. Scott Lowery will set you up in the office and take care of anything you need while you're there."

"Thank you." Landon stood up, feeling a little lightheaded.

As he made his way back to his own office, he wasn't nervous about the research of the company, or about traveling, or about meeting with the clients.

The only thought in his mind was that he would miss taking Carter to soccer practice.

20

Hailey stared at the TV screen Wednesday night. There was a sitcom playing at a low volume, but it didn't matter. She wasn't paying attention anyway.

The kids had been in bed for almost an hour, the kitchen was clean, and the laundry was folded. She could enjoy a movie or read a book, but her mind wouldn't focus on anything. Landon had said he would call tonight, but so far she hadn't heard from him.

She sighed as she rose from the couch, thinking maybe she should just go to bed.

Just then her phone rang. The sudden sound startled her, and her heart pounded as she grabbed the phone and pressed the button. "Hello?"

"Hey," Landon said.

"Hey," she replied, sinking back down on the couch. She wanted to melt into his embrace at the sound of his voice.

"How are you?" he asked.

"I'm fine. How are you? You sound tired." Hailey's forehead creased with concern.

"Well, I am. My flight was at six this morning, and I barely slept last night. I was still trying to go over my notes until midnight."

"I know. I'm sorry. It seems a little ridiculous that they made this trip with such short notice."

"Yeah, but you know that's how it goes. Mr. Benton decides when he decides, and when he says jump, I say how high."

She sighed. "I know. I'm just sorry that you're tired."

"And I'm sorry that I'm in Dallas and not there in Twin Creeks."

"Me too."

Landon fell quiet for a moment, and Hailey could hear the sound of papers rustling.

"Are you still working?"

"Kind of," he said. "I got takeout for the hotel, and I'm just making sure the presentation is ready for in the morning."

"I should let you go then," Hailey said.

"I'm sorry, Hailey. I wanted to talk longer."

She waved a hand in the air as if he could see her. "It's okay. I understand." She did understand, but that didn't mean she liked it.

"I'll call you tomorrow when I'm on the way to the airport."

"Okay," she said as confidently as she could.

"Goodnight, Hailey."

"Goodnight, Landon." She hung onto the phone for a moment and then dropped it onto the couch pillow. "That was disappointing," she said to no one. "Oh well, he's got work to do. And the job comes first." It had to, didn't it? They weren't married or engaged. He wasn't really their family. So when the company wanted him to jump on a plane, that was his first priority.

So why did it bother her so much?

His voice had sounded distant, and she knew he was staring at work papers, even as he talked to her. "Get over it, Hailey," she told herself. "He's just tired and busy with work. He'll be home tomorrow night, and you can talk then."

But he wasn't home the next night. As Hailey was standing on the sideline at Carter's soccer practice, watching the assistant coach try unsuccessfully to wrangle the boys, her phone buzzed with a text.

Hey, I'm sorry. I know I said I would call on my way to the airport, but I'm not flying out tonight. The presentation went well, and the clients wanted to go to lunch. Then the team met in the afternoon and worked late to get their revisions done before tomorrow. I'm staying another day. Maybe two. Not sure.

Hailey's heart sank as Charlotte and Ellie tugged on her arms and said they were hungry for the hundredth time. She hadn't gotten dinner ready before practice, so they would have to eat afterward. "Just a few more minutes," she told them. But in her mind, she couldn't focus on dinner. How much longer would Landon be gone? She shook her head, reminding herself she wasn't supposed to depend on him. He had his work, and this was her responsibility. Yes, it was nice to have his help, but once again, she had to handle the kids and their life on her own.

21

L andon couldn't remember when he'd been so tired. Thursday's meeting had turned into three days of meetings with the clients and the team in Dallas. The company loved his ideas, and they wanted to move forward as quickly as possible. Landon was thrilled, but they wanted to make a few changes, and sign contracts on Monday. Landon had worked non-stop through Saturday afternoon until he boarded the plane to Tennessee. They wanted him to stay for the contract signing Monday morning, but he declined, saying the team could handle it.

All he wanted to do was get back to Twin Creeks.

Now it was Sunday morning, and he would guess he'd had five hours of sleep. After his flight was delayed, and his bags were lost, he finally made it home after midnight. He had barely remembered to text Hailey to let her know he'd arrived before his head hit the pillow.

No matter how tired he was, he wasn't going to miss church this morning. He hurried through the foyer, even though he was at least five minutes late. He glanced at his watch. Make that ten minutes. Moving through the sanctuary doors, he glanced around to see where Hailey and the kids were. He grimaced when he saw they were all the way down front. He pasted on a smile and moved down the aisle as the church sang a worship song.

He tried not to worry, but was everyone really staring at him as he walked right to Hailey's row and squeezed past the kids to sit by her? Once in the row, he met her eyes and mouthed, "Hi." He wanted to wrap her in a hug right then and there, but he restrained himself.

Hailey responded with a small wave, but she didn't smile like she had before. Maybe she was just tired. He knew Carter had a soccer game yesterday, and Charlotte had an afternoon gymnastics meet. That was a lot to handle on her own.

Inwardly, he groaned that he hadn't been there, but what could he do? He couldn't exactly tell Mr. Benton, sorry I can't go to Texas. That just wasn't what he did. Not if he liked his job and wanted to be promoted. As the final notes of the song played, the pastor walked on stage and motioned for everyone to sit down.

Landon sat down next to Hailey, with Carter on his other side. He told himself not to think about the weekend and focus on the message. There would be plenty of time to spend with Hailey and the kids later this afternoon. He put his hand to his mouth to cover a yawn. No, he couldn't do that. He hadn't even unpacked his suitcase, and he had to get ready for the week ahead. He sighed. Hailey would understand if he needed to catch up today, and then he could go over for dinner after work Monday. They could talk then.

As hard as he tried, he couldn't focus on the sermon. He stared at the words in the Bible on his lap as the pastor read them, but it wasn't sinking in. This wasn't who he was. He hated giving less than his best to anything, especially to church. But the best he could do was try to keep his eyes open.

After the final prayer, the pastor dismissed the congregation. Landon turned to Hailey. How was it possible he was sitting next to her, but felt so far away?

"Hey," she said.

"Hey," he replied, but that was the only word he got out before Carter tugged on his arm and started telling him about the soccer game.

Landon smiled and nodded, giving the boy his attention. When Carter took a breath after telling Landon about the two goals he scored, Landon looked back at Hailey.

"How was your day?"

Hailey took in a big breath and blew it out. "Busy," she said. "Good, though. Carter played great, and Charlotte had her best meet yet."

Landon frowned. "I'm sorry I missed it."

Hailey shrugged. "It's alright. You couldn't help it."

Landon nodded. "Right. But I'm here now."

"Do you want to come over for lunch?"

Landon covered another yawn. "I would love to. But I barely slept, and I don't know if I'll be very good company. Plus I've got some things I need to do around the house. What if I come over for dinner tomorrow night?"

He saw the disappointment in Hailey's eyes before she dropped her gaze to the floor. "Sure. I know you're tired."

Landon wasn't sure what to say next. He wanted to take her hand in his and say he knew she was tired too. But what would the kids say? And what would the church members surrounding them think if they saw him holding her hand? Everyone here had known Kyle. It was surprising enough that he was sitting next to her in church. He didn't need to give people something to talk about. He cleared his throat. "I'm sorry. I wish I could."

"It's okay. Kids, say bye to Landon. We need to get home."

Each of the kids said goodbye to him as they moved out of the pew. Landon watched them go, and Hailey turned back to wave, but didn't say anything else.

He sighed just before another yawn escaped. It was true, he wouldn't be any good to anybody until he got some sleep.

Still, as he walked up the aisle and out of church, he couldn't help but think of all he had missed over the weekend. And if he had to travel again, he wondered how much more he would miss in the days to come.

22

L andon beamed with pride as he walked into Mr. Benton's office on Monday morning. He didn't have to wait long, since he had an email Sunday night that Mr. Benton wanted to see him first thing in the morning.

"Richards," Mr. Benton practically yelled. "You're amazing. I haven't stopped hearing about you since Thursday morning. Scott said you were on fire!"

Landon felt his cheeks flush as he took a seat. "Thank you, sir. It was a lot of work, but we pulled it off."

"Don't be modest. Hoffman Hotels was floored with your presentation. I've never seen a client want to sign paperwork so fast."

"They did seem pretty eager."

"And you managed to get it all on their practically impossible time table. All while working out of a temp office and sleeping in a hotel room."

"Well, to be honest, I barely left the office."

"I'm sure you didn't," Mr. Benton laughed. "I have to

tell you. I've been in this business a long time and not a lot impresses me. But, Richards, I'm impressed. I knew you would do a good job, but this was completely above and beyond. You knocked it out of the park."

"Thank you. I'm glad everyone is happy. And honestly, I'm a little relieved it's done. It was quick and a lot of work. But I know the team in Dallas will handle the rest of it with no problems."

Mr. Benton clapped his hands together. A sure sign that something big was coming. Landon braced himself.

"That's exactly why I called you in here. Scott has been doing a great job at the Dallas office, but it's growing and we need more leadership there. We would like to make you Vice President of Client Relations with a permanent move to Dallas."

Landon felt like he'd had the wind knocked out of him.

"What?" he managed to say as he gasped.

Mr. Benton laughed. "Surprised, I guess. You heard me, right. A move to Dallas and the promotion you've been dreaming of. We've been looking across the company for the right man, and we're confident it's you. We'll give you a few weeks, a month if you need it, to finish up with clients here and set up housing in Dallas. They'll have your new office ready for you there. I hate to lose you in our office, since I've gotten used to seeing you. But I know you'll do great things there."

Landon could hear Mr. Benton's voice while he kept his eyes on him, but his mind was running circles. How could he move to Dallas? He'd lived in Tennessee his whole life. But wasn't this what he had been working toward for so many years? He had to do it, didn't he?

Only one image kept flashing across his mind. What would Hailey's face look like if he told her? He squeezed his eyes shut, opened them again, and saw Mr. Benton standing to shake his hand.

Landon stood too and reached across the table. "Thank you," he said and turned to go. He wasn't really sure Mr. Benton was done talking, but he had to get out of that room.

In his office, he paced back and forth, alternating putting his hands on his hips, then his forehead. How could he do this? How could he tell Hailey? How could he go?

Finally, he collapsed into his chair. "God," he said out loud, not caring who heard him. "Why is this happening now? A year ago I would have been screaming from the rooftops about this. I would have run home and started packing. But now?" He let his face fall into his hands. "Now what do I do?" He had run through ten different scenarios in his mind, but, so far, none of them worked the way he wanted. "God, I don't know what to do. And I don't know how I can face Hailey and tell her this news. Lord, I need Your help." Hailey's own words came to mind. *God is always there to lead and direct us. If you focus on Him, instead of an earthly man, you'll be headed in the right direction.*

He took a deep breath and blew it out. "Ok, God, I'm asking You to show me the way. I'll trust You in where You lead me."

He hoped God had an answer because, right now, Landon couldn't see which way to go if his life depended on it. And right now, it felt like it did.

23

"We need to talk," Landon said on Monday night after dinner.

Hailey smiled at him from where she stood finishing up the dishes. The kids had just gone off to play in their rooms, and she felt like she could finally breathe. The weekend had been long and exhausting, and when Landon didn't come over after church, she had to admit she had been upset. But now that he was here, laughing and talking with the kids as they all ate dinner together, everything felt right again.

"Okay," she said, moving to the couch next to him. She took a seat, and he glanced towards the hallway before he took her hands in his. His touch warmed her heart, and she looked into his eyes as he spoke.

"Mr. Benton called me into his office this morning. They've offered me a promotion. Vice President of Client Relations."

Hailey's mouth dropped open. "Really? Landon! That's incredible!"

He cleared his throat and ran a thumb over the back of her hand. "Thank you. I'm honored."

"This is what you've always wanted."

He nodded. "Yes it is. But there's something else."

Hailey's heart skipped a beat, and she swallowed before she said, "What is it?"

"The position is in Texas."

Hailey gasped quietly, and she pulled her hands from him as they flew to her mouth. "You're moving?" The words echoed painfully in her soul.

Landon was silent for a few moments as they sat on the couch.

"You're moving to Texas," she repeated, trying to keep her voice down so the kids wouldn't hear from their rooms.

He sighed and shook his head. "I don't know what to do. That's what they want me to do. It's a promotion that I've been working toward for a long time. Ever since I started working there, really."

Hailey stood and walked to the kitchen. She couldn't sit there and listen to this. Tears stung at her eyes. Could he really leave now? After everything they'd been through? She had tried to keep from getting her feelings involved, but now it was too late. Reaching in the cabinet, she grabbed a glass and filled it with water. Drinking it gave her time to think, but before she was finished, Landon was at her side.

"I didn't want to tell you. I wish I could pretend like it didn't happen. I'm happy here, and I would be happy staying here and working in my current position." When she didn't turn to face him, he leaned on the counter and put one hand over his face. "I'm sorry. I don't know what to say."

"What are we going to do?"

Landon looked up when she said "We." For a second he looked hopeful, but then his face fell. "I've always known it was possible that if I moved up in the company it would require a move. It always seemed exciting, and I thought I would enjoy moving and trying out a new city." He reached for her hand again. "But I've never been a part of a 'we' before, and now I don't know what to do."

"Do you want to go?" Hailey asked as she bit her lip.

Landon shook his head. "I don't know."

"But you do want the promotion?"

He lowered his eyes. "Yes, I do."

Hailey summoned all the courage she could find. "It's okay, Landon."

He looked up at her, and his eyes held a touch of hope. "Really?"

"I know you've wanted this and worked so hard to get here. You're good at your job, and you spent a long time focusing on your career." She paused and swallowed to push down the emotion. "You don't have to worry about us. I know you promised Kyle you would help us and look out for us. You've been so helpful the last few months, and now I see that I can make it after all. You've given me time to find joy again, and I will always be grateful for that. But you have your career to think about. We will be okay."

"Hailey," Landon started, but she held up her hand.

"No, let's not do this. You were right to take things slowly and be careful. Now we don't have to have any regrets. You can go, Landon. It's what you've worked for, and now you've earned it. I'm so happy for you, truly. I know you'll do great. But please, make it easier on both of us, and let's just let it go."

"That's not what I want," he said with desperation in his voice.

"Do you want to give up your job?"

Landon met her gaze, and his eyes pleaded with her not to ask him that. But in the end, he shrugged.

"I know you don't. And that means the only option is to go. The kids and I have our lives here, and now your life is taking you somewhere else. I don't like it, but I think the only thing to do right now is let it go." She set the glass in the sink and turned and walked to the living room. "I'm tired, and I don't want either of us to get emotional and say something we don't mean. Let's just say goodnight and see you later."

Landon opened his mouth as if he wanted to argue, but then he sighed, resigned that she was right. "See you later, Hailey."

"See you later, Landon."

She watched him turn and walk out the door, like he had so many times over the last few months. As she sank onto the couch, she pictured the first time he had come to the house and said he wanted to help her out. It was the night he had taken Carter to soccer practice, and the two of them had come back into the house like fast friends.

Landon had brought life back into their house, and she would be forever grateful for that.

But as she realized she wouldn't see him walking back in that door, the tears came. Tears of sadness for everything they would miss. As she thought about the kids, new waves of sorrow rolled over her, and she covered her mouth to keep the sob in her throat from bursting out.

Hailey let the tears roll down her cheeks, thinking of the memories they had made. Months ago, she was just relieved to have a second set of hands to help. Now she felt like her heart was being ripped from her chest for the second time in her life.

"God," she whispered through her tears. "Help me. I know You used Landon to show me that I could still live life. Give me strength now. The Lord gives, and the Lord takes away. Give me the peace to see that this was for a season, and help me to walk with You even when he's gone."

Hailey went to bed and fell asleep praying the same prayer, and crying the same tears.

24

L andon stood in an empty apartment and turned around looking at the bare walls. It was smaller than his house in Twin Creeks, and the cost of living in Dallas was higher too. But what did he need a big place for? His new job would take even more time than before, and he would spend most of his time at the office.

And it wasn't like he had a family to house.

The only family he had ever wanted was in Tennessee.

He turned to the property manager standing in the doorway. "I'll take it," he said. "Can I move in on the first?"

"Absolutely, let's just get you to sign the paperwork."

Landon nodded and followed the woman back to the apartment office. The first would give him three weeks to pack up and move. His boss had said he could have a month, and it had only been four days. Of course, he should have known they would ask him to fly out today to meet with his new boss and spend a few days getting to know the new office. He was still coping with the idea of moving, and now he would spend his weekend in a strange city where he knew no one.

At least it gave him a chance to find a place to live. Now that he'd done that, he could head to the office for the lunch meeting Scott had set up.

Once the paperwork was finished, he had nothing else to do but drive to the office. He turned his thoughts to the job. If he could focus on work and dive into his new role, maybe he could keep himself from thinking about Hailey and the kids.

And that was the best thing to do, wasn't it? Hailey said they needed a clean break. He planned to go over and tell the kids goodbye before he left permanently, so they would know he was moving and not that he stopped coming by for no reason. But he hadn't even heard from Hailey. When he walked out of her house and the door closed behind him, it felt like the end of that story.

Landon sighed as he turned his car onto the interstate toward the office. This would be the new path he would take to work. It was a different one than he had taken since he first started with the company. He should be excited about a new opportunity and ready to tackle the new job.

Instead, all he could think about was the pit in his stomach. The one that told him he was making a terrible mistake.

~

HAILEY SMILED AND WAVED AS THE KIDS WALKED TOWARD the school. She kept up the fake happy persona until they had turned and were out of sight.

She had made a promise to herself that she wouldn't fall back into the darkness she had lived in before, and she was doing the best she could to keep spirits high for the kids.

But that didn't mean she wasn't hurting inside. She was the one who had told Landon they needed to say see you later that night and move on, and she had meant it. But as one week turned into two without so much as a text message from him, she began to wonder if there had really been anything between them at all.

The kids had been upset when she sat them down and explained Landon was moving away. She promised he cared about them and would come by to say goodbye before he moved, but he would probably be very busy until then.

Carter was taking it the hardest of all. He mentioned at least once a day that soccer practice wouldn't be any fun without Landon.

Hailey sighed as she drove toward work. If she was honest, she would have to admit that a lot of life was more fun with Landon around.

"God," she began to pray as she had made a habit of doing the last few weeks. "Thank You for today. I pray that You will be with the kids today, watch over them, and keep them safe. Watch over me too, and, Lord, please lead me today. I was so lost without Kyle, then I found my way. It was only surviving, but I was doing okay. When Landon came around, everything changed again, for the better.

God, I know You have a plan, and I want to trust You. Help my heart as I get used to doing things without him. Thank You that even though he isn't here, You are. Thank You for never leaving me alone. And God, I pray that You will be with Landon as he moves to Texas. Give him a wonderful and happy life. I pray that You will bless him." She stopped short of praying that God would make a way for Landon to come back into her life. That wasn't something she was going to ask for.

Even though it was the one thing she really wanted.

25

L andon stuffed his hands in his pockets as he walked across the parking lot in silence. His duffle bag from the weekend was still in his backseat, since he'd driven straight here from the airport. The asphalt parking lot changed to grass under his feet, and he took a deep breath and blew it out.

He hadn't been here in a long time. Not since the funeral. His heart pounded at a deafening rhythm in his ears as he moved past the gravestones. He hadn't planned to come here, but when he picked up his car after the flight, something drew him here. Maybe it was time.

Slowly he moved through the cemetery, even though he wanted to come, now it felt like his shoes were made of lead as he neared the grave site. Sooner than he wanted it to, the headstone came into view, and he stopped at the foot as he read the words. "Kyle Peterson, loving husband, devoted father."

Landon could have added two more words: "Best Friend."

"God," he prayed. "I could really use some advice right now. In the past, Kyle would be the one I asked. He counseled me about work, financial decisions, what house to buy, and everything else. I never asked him about relationships though. There was never anything to ask. I said I wasn't going to get married or have a family, and I meant it." He shook his head. "Maybe that was dumb. I saw how happy Kyle was. He had everything. The career, the family, and he made sacrifices, but they were always the right ones. I've made sacrifices, but maybe that wasn't right. I've only made sacrifices to work more. I've never said no to the company because my job was what mattered."

He ran his fingers through his hair and over his beard that desperately needed a trim. "God, I don't know what to do. I've waited a long time for this promotion, and I've always been willing to move if necessary. So why is this happening now, just when I wanted to stay put?"

He turned and put his hands on his hips as he slowly paced back and forth. His mind reeled with thoughts of work, and Texas, and Hailey and the kids, until he let out a groan. Turning back to the grave stone, he spoke again.

"I know Kyle isn't here, but I wish I could talk to him. I know he's in a better place. God, I don't know why he would ask me to watch over his family if something happened to him. He couldn't have really known that he wouldn't always be here. But God, You did. You knew exactly the length of his life, and You were the one who had him ask me. You were the one who had me make a promise to look after them." He took a deep breath. "You were the one who prompted Hailey to call me that day to pick up Carter. You've always known the whole story, even though I can only see one part."

He paused and turned his gaze from the grave up to the sky. "You knew all of Kyle's life, every single day. And he lived his life to the fullest. He didn't miss a chance to be a good friend, or to see his kids. He took every opportunity to have fun and used his time to help others." He sighed. "I admit that I wish I was more like Kyle. But maybe that's not the best goal. God, I have spent a lot of my life looking out for myself. I've worried about my career, my house, my car, and my life. But you've called me to more than that, and I want to follow You. God, I made a promise to Kyle, but before that I made a commitment to You. You are God, and You have a plan for my life." He turned his palms towards the sky and held out his hands. "I'm Yours. I will follow what You have for me, and I will trust that what You have for me is best." He squeezed his eyes closed and prayed quietly. "Heavenly Father, please show me what to do now."

In the quiet of the moment, a peace filled his soul as he knew what his next step was. A happy sigh escaped his lips. "God, none of this is what I would have expected. Not now, and not ever. But here I am. And now I will follow You into the future You have planned."

He opened his eyes and slowly walked forward. Putting his hand on the gravestone, he spoke. "Goodbye, my friend. I'll always miss you. Thanks for being the best example and teaching me the most important lesson in life."

Turning away, he slowly walked to his car. He would still carry the sadness and loss of Kyle, but now he knew what he was supposed to do.

26

Hailey slid the casserole into the oven and glanced at the clock, making a mental note of what time it needed to come out. As she wiped her hands on a nearby towel, a knock sounded at the door. The kids were watching TV and must not have heard it, since they didn't go thundering to the door fighting over who was going to open it.

With a sigh, she made her way over and peeked through the window. She gasped at the sight. Placing her hand to her heart that was beating at a ridiculous speed, she told herself to walk slowly and calmly to the door.

Landon was here.

As she reached for the doorknob, she remembered that he was probably here to say his goodbyes to the kids. Still, she couldn't help but long for one moment alone with him. She slipped out and pulled the door shut behind her, before the kids could notice.

When she looked up, she met his eyes and was sure she was going to melt right there on the doorstep. Only when she looked up did she realize he was holding a bouquet of flowers.

"Hailey," he said.

The sound of her name on his lips brought tears to her eyes. "Hi," she managed to say.

"I've missed you," he blurted out.

She blinked rapidly. "I've missed you too." She cleared her throat and told herself to focus, before she said more than she intended. "I wondered if you were still going to come say goodbye. Are you all ready to go?"

Landon stepped close and stopped only a few inches from her. "I would never leave without saying goodbye."

She looked down at the ground and reached behind her for the doorknob. "The kids will be glad to see you."

Landon reached for her arm to stop her and heat ran through the ends of her fingertips. "I'll be thrilled to see them. But I wanted to see you first."

Hailey finally dared to look him in the eyes. "Okay," she said.

"These are for you." He held up the flowers. "I wanted you to always remember this day."

Hailey bit her lip. She would never forget a moment with him, but today was a day she wasn't sure she wanted to live on in her memory. Still, it was nice that he wanted her to have something to remember him by. "Thank you," she said around the lump in her throat.

"Hailey, I'm sorry that I ever let you think I could leave you."

"What?" she asked, not sure she had understood.

"I can't leave you. Not you, or the kids. I just can't do it. I don't want to."

His arms went around her waist, and she placed her hands on both of his arms. "What are you saying?"

"I'm saying I want you. I want life with you. You're the best thing that ever happened to me. I've avoided relationships for so long because I was sure that I would get hurt, and because I was sure I could make it just fine on my own. But the truth is, I don't want to be on my own. I want a family. You and Carter and Charlotte and Ellie, you're the family that I want."

"Landon..." Hailey tried to stop him, but he shook his head and continued.

"I've put my career first for such a long time, because it was the only thing that mattered to me. Everything has changed now. I don't care about a job, or a career, the most important thing to me is to see you smile. Hailey, you have the most beautiful smile. But for too long, you didn't smile. You were sad, and rightfully so. I never set out to win your heart. But I'm here to say that's exactly what I want to do. Hailey, you are an incredible woman. You are beautiful, and funny, and fun, and smart, and capable. You survived something that would have broken other women, and I'm forever sorry you had to go through that. But in the midst of it, we found a bond and a connection I've never known before. I don't want to lose that. And your kids are the world to me. I want to teach them and to watch them grow and learn. I don't know anything about being a dad, but a wise woman once told me that if I follow the example of our heavenly Father, I'll be headed in the right direction."

Hailey smiled. "That's true."

Landon stepped back and took her hands in his. "Will

you give me that chance? Will you let me be the one to make you smile again? Will you let me be the one to walk with you as we follow God into whatever He has for us? Hailey, will you marry me?"

Hailey gasped as he reached into his pocket and pulled out a small black box from his pocket. He opened it to reveal a shining diamond ring.

"Landon," she said, barely able to speak. "You are the most unexpected thing that's ever happened to me. I trusted God to lead me in the next step, and now I know exactly what that is. Yes, yes! I'll marry you!"

He took her in his arms. Then, for just a moment, he gazed into her eyes, and the connection between them was solidified. The connection grew as the moment lingered. Landon took her face in his hand and held it gently. Her skin tingled at his touch as he slowly lowered his lips to hers. Hailey stretched up on her tiptoes to meet him and wrapped her arms around his waist. His lips were soft and gentle as he kissed her again and again. His hand moved from her face down to her back where he made slow circles. She drank in the sweetness of the kiss, and all the promise it held.

Raising his lips from hers, Landon gazed into her eyes before brushing one last gentle kiss on her forehead. Hailey was breathless as she looked up at him.

Landon closed the ring box. The kiss had almost made her forget about it entirely. "I know you might not be ready to wear this yet. You can keep it somewhere safe until you're ready to tell the kids. But I hope you know I'm ready when you are. I want to tell the whole world that we're going to spend our lives together."

Hailey smiled at him, the biggest smile she had. "Thank you for understanding. I won't make you wait long, but we do need to explain it to them first."

Landon nodded. "Of course."

"What did you tell them at work?"

"I spoke with Mr. Benton. Honestly, I was sure he was going to let me go. But I told him I was thrilled with the opportunity and honored to have been chosen. But the truth was, I couldn't take the promotion at this time. If they would have me, I said I would like to stay with the company in my current position, but that I can't commit to being in the office like I have been in the past. I need more time to spend with my family."

"Really?" Hailey asked.

"Yes, really."

"And what did he say?"

Landon blew out a breath. "He wasn't happy about it. I might have a ways to go before I make it back into his good graces, but he let me keep my job. I think he wants me to stay, even though it's not exactly what he wanted me to do. I don't care, though. I'm happy to have a job, but he's not the person I'm worried about making happy. I want to do what God wants me to do, and I want to be with you and the kids, nothing else matters."

EPILOGUE

Hailey and Landon sat on the couch next to each other. They were closer than they had ever dared be in front of the kids. It had only been two days since Landon had proposed, but she knew she would burst if she had to keep it inside any longer.

After their time on the porch, Landon had slipped in the door and waited for the kids to notice him. Carter was the first one to see him and jumped up like he had been shot out of his chair by a rocket.

Hailey had laughed as the kids hugged him and spoke all at once trying to tell him the things he had missed.

Now she sat on the couch with him, happy to know that he wouldn't miss anything any more.

"Hey, guys, can everybody come sit down for a minute? Your mom and I have something to tell you," Landon said.

Hailey's heart beat at double speed. She couldn't wait to tell them, but it would still take some getting used to hearing Landon talk about them as a unit.

"What is it?" Carter yelled as he jumped on his knees onto the couch next to Landon.

"You have to sit to find out."

Charlotte and Ellie giggled as they scooted close to Hailey. "We're sitting!" Charlotte announced.

Landon took in a deep breath and blew it out as he looked at Hailey. He smiled. "You ready?"

"Yes," she said confidently.

"You know guys that I care about all of you, right?"

The kids bobbed their heads up and down, impatient for the news.

"I'm thankful that God made us friends, and that He let me get to know you and become part of your family. But I want to make that official. Your mom and I have been spending a lot of time together, and we've talked a lot about how we feel and about our future." He paused and looked at each of them before he continued. "So we wanted to tell you that we've decided we want to all be a family together, and I've asked your mom to marry me."

The girls gasped and looked at Hailey.

Carter jumped off the couch and yelled, "What?"

"Mommy, what did you say?" asked Ellie, ever so sweetly.

Hailey smiled at her and cupped her chin in her hand. "I said yes."

"Really?" Charlotte asked.

"Really."

"Does that mean Landon will be with us all the time? Carter asked.

"Yes, it does," Landon said. "After we get married, we will all live together."

The kids all jumped up and down and squealed at that news.

"Oh, Mom," Charlotte said. "I'm so happy. It's just like Landon said at dinner that time. We never stopped being a family. And now we get to be an even bigger family with Landon."

Hailey's eyes filled with tears, but she smiled through them as she looked at her daughter. "That's right, sweetie. Mommy loves you so much, and you know your daddy loved you more than anything. And now Landon gets to love you too."

Charlotte wiped at a single tear trailing down her cheek before she wrapped her arms around Hailey.

Carter was already hugging Landon, maybe a little too tight as he spoke at top volume about all the fun things they could do together. Ellie had sandwiched herself in between them and was giggling.

Hailey glanced at Landon as if to say, "Are you sure?"

He laughed as he looked at her and leaned over the top of the kids and kissed her. "I could never have asked for anything more than this," he said.

"Welcome to the family, Landon."

He winked at her. "Welcome to your new happily ever after, Hailey."

ABOUT THE AUTHOR

Hannah Jo Abbott is not just a writer, but a wife, a mom of four, a homeschool teacher, a daughter, a sister, and a friend. She loves writing stories about life, love, and the grace of God. She finds inspiration and encouragement from reading the stories others share. Hannah lives with her husband and children in Sweet Home Alabama.

For updates on her writing and to receive a FREE novella, sign up for Hannah Jo's newsletters at www.hannahjoabbott.com

facebook.com/hjabooks
instagram.com/hannahjoabbottwriter

ALSO BY HANNAH JO ABBOTT

Whispering Oaks Ranch Series:

Hope for the Cowboy

Courage for the Cowboy

Match for the Cowboy

Dream for the Cowboy

Sweet Home Billionaire Series:

Small Town Billionaire

Hometown Billionaire

Downtown Billionaire

Faith and Love Series:

Walk with Me

Dream with me

Stay with Me

Come with Me

Love Off Limits Series:

Her Best Friend

Her Roommate's Brother

Her Brother's Best Friend

His Daughter's Teacher

Her Sister's Ex

His Best Friend's Widow

Heroes of Freedom Ridge Series:

Stranded with The Hero

Trusting The Hero

Running to the Hero

Billionaire for Christmas Series:

Billionaire Under the Mistletoe

Billionaire at The Christmas Inn